S0-AFI-148

Katie shook her head. "Having toe shoes doesn't prove anything. Anyone can buy a pair. There's only one way I'll believe Jillian took pointe."

"What's that?" Megan asked.

"I want to see her dance," Katie said.

"I'll dance for you," I said. "It's no big deal."

"I'll believe it when I see it," Katie said. "Come on, you guys. Let's go."

After the others were gone, I walked down to the dressing room. All the other kids had left. Giselle, the ballet-school cat, rubbed up against my ankles while I stared into the mirror. I had two big problems:

1. I didn't own toe shoes. (And I had no idea where to get a pair.)

2. Even if I did find a pair of toe shoes, I didn't know how to dance in them.

I scooped up Giselle and buried my face in her fur.

"Mrrw," Giselle said.

"Help," I whispered back.

Don't miss any of the books in
this fabulous new series!

#1 Becky at the Barre

Coming soon:

#3 Katie's Last Class
#4 Megan's Nutcracker Prince

And look for PONY CAMP —
a great new series from HarperPaperbacks.

ATTENTION: ORGANIZATIONS AND CORPORATIONS

Most HarperPaperbacks are available at special quantity
discounts for bulk purchases for sales promotions, premiums,
or fund-raising. For information, please call or write:
**Special Markets Department, HarperCollins Publishers,
10 East 53rd Street, New York, N.Y. 10022
Telephone: (212) 207-7528. Fax: (212) 207-7222.**

Jillian On Her Toes

Written by

Emily Costello

Illustrated by

Marcy Ramsey

HarperPaperbacks

A Division of HarperCollins*Publishers*

If you purchased this book without a cover, you should be aware that this book is stolen property. It was reported as "unsold and destroyed" to the publisher and neither the author nor the publisher has received any payment for this "stripped book."

This is a work of fiction. The characters, incidents, and dialogues are products of the author's imagination and are not to be construed as real. Any resemblance to actual events or persons, living or dead, is entirely coincidental.

HarperPaperbacks *A Division of* HarperCollins*Publishers*
10 East 53rd Street, New York, N.Y. 10022

Copyright © 1994 by Daniel Weiss Associates, Inc., and Emily Costello
Cover art copyright © 1994 Daniel Weiss Associates, Inc.

All rights reserved. No part of this book may be used or reproduced in any manner whatsoever without written permission of the publisher, except in the case of brief quotations embodied in critical articles and reviews. For information address Daniel Weiss Associates, Inc., 33 West 17th Street, New York, New York 10011.

Produced by Daniel Weiss Associates, Inc., 33 West 17th Street, New York, New York 10011.

First printing: June 1994

Printed in the United States of America

HarperPaperbacks and colophon are trademarks of HarperCollins*Publishers*

10 9 8 7 6 5 4 3 2 1

To Eric, with a big smack on the lips.

One

Odd One Out

"Next group!" Pat, my ballet teacher, called out.

I stepped forward. So did Megan Isozaki and Becky Hill. We stood in fifth position and waited for the music to begin.

While we were waiting, Becky whispered something to Megan. They giggled. But they didn't share the secret with me. That made me feel terrible. I wanted Megan and Becky to be my friends.

The music began. Megan and Becky and I moved forward. As soon as I started to dance, I forgot about the other girls and their secret.

Ballet takes concentration. *Tons* of concentration. When I'm dancing, I can't think about anything else. I can't worry about my friends or my parents.

I did the last step of the combination.

"Don't forget to point your toes, Jillian," Pat said.

Jillian—that's me. My whole name is Jillian Kormach. I'm nine years old. I am African-American. I have light-brown skin and long curly hair. My eyes are dark brown.

I frowned at Pat. I know it's important for her to correct me. If she didn't, I would never get better. But that doesn't mean I have to like it. Besides, I think my toes were pointed plenty. I learned how to do that in one of my very first ballet classes.

"Take a quick break, everyone," Pat said.

Becky started to show Risa Cumberland how to do a jump Pat had taught us that afternoon.

Charlotte Stype and Lynn Frazier headed for the drinking fountain in the hallway.

Dean Stellar was talking to Megan. (I think he has a crush on her.)

Philip—Dean's twin brother—was bragging to Kim Woyczek about something. Probably football. That's all Philip is interested in. Kim looked bored.

I knew how Kim felt. I was bored, too. I didn't have anyone to talk to. The people in my class acted as if they didn't know I was alive.

Nikki Norg said something to Megan. Then she walked over to where I was standing by the mirror. She frowned at her reflection. Most of Nikki's hair had come out of her bun.

Nikki's light-brown hair is extremely long and

curly. When she wears it down, it falls to the middle of her back. It looks beautiful that way. But we have to wear our hair in a bun during ballet class. Nikki's hair won't stay up. She spends half of class trying to get it to behave.

"You're going to need partners after the break," Pat announced. "Dean, I want you to dance with Charlotte. Let her know when she comes back from the drinking fountain. Philip, you're with Becky. John, please dance with Risa."

Pat always picks partners for the boys in our class. She wants to make sure they dance with one of us girls. Pat lets the rest of us pair up on our own.

I glanced at Nikki. I was hoping she would ask me to be her partner. She didn't. But she didn't ask anyone else either.

Nikki noticed I was watching her. Our eyes met.

I smiled.

Nikki smiled back.

That had to mean we were going to be partners!

I felt great.

I always panic when Pat has us pair up. See, I just moved here. I haven't made any friends yet. That makes picking partners hard.

I was born in Brooklyn—that's a part of New York City. I lived there until about three months ago.

Then my whole life changed.

3

My mom and dad got divorced. A few months after that, Mom and I moved to Glory, Washington.

Glory is a tiny town near Seattle. My mom grew up here. We are living with my grandparents.

The first month I was here, I was not very friendly. I was too busy being angry with my parents—especially my mother. By the time I cooled off, I wasn't the "new girl" anymore. The other kids were used to seeing me alone. Maybe they thought I liked it.

But for the last two months, I had been trying to make friends. I smiled all the time. I laughed when the other kids made jokes. (Even if they weren't telling them to me.) But it wasn't working. I was beginning to think I was invisible to the kids in Glory.

That's why I was so happy Nikki smiled at me. I hoped it meant she was starting to like me.

Nikki pinned her hair back into a bun.

"My hair drives me crazy," Nikki said.

"I think it's pretty," I said. "It's so long."

"I've never gotten it cut," Nikki told me.

"Never?" I asked.

Nikki shook her head. The movement made her hair fall down again.

I laughed.

Nikki stomped her foot. "I *hate* my hair!"

"Maybe you should cut it off," I suggested.

"Good idea," Nikki said.

"Places, everyone," Pat called. "Let's go!"

Megan hurried over to us. Megan is in my class at regular school. She's half-Irish and half-Japanese. Megan has long brownish-black hair with gold highlights. She is skinny. Megan is one of the nicest girls in Glory.

"Hi, Megan," I said. (See? I was *trying* to be friendly.)

"Hi!" she answered. "Hey, Nikki."

"Howdy, partner," Nikki greeted Megan.

My heart sank. Nikki didn't want to be my partner. She was going to dance with Megan. That made sense. Megan and Nikki were almost always partners.

I shook my head. I'm really stupid sometimes. I glanced around the studio. Who was I going to dance with now?

Kim caught my eye. Kim goes to my school, but she's a grade ahead of me. I don't know her very well. But I do know ballet can't be much fun for her. Kim is an okay dancer. But she is also overweight. Some of the kids in Pat's class make fun of her. I don't care that Kim is fat. I'm always happy to dance with her.

I headed in Kim's direction. But just then, Kim noticed that Lynn needed a partner. She ran over and stood next to her.

All of the kids seemed to be paired up. But that

was impossible. There are exactly twelve kids in my class. Even though I'm usually the last person to find a partner, someone always ends up dancing with me.

Then I realized Katie Ruiz was absent. That meant there was an uneven number of kids in class. Everyone but me had a partner. I was the odd one out. I felt like crying.

"Who doesn't have a partner?" Pat asked.

I didn't feel like answering. I was too embarrassed.

"Jillian doesn't," Charlotte yelled.

I gave Charlotte a nasty look. I don't like her. I could tell she was happy to see I was the most unpopular person in the class.

"Jillian, why don't you come up here and dance with me?" Pat suggested.

I made a face. I couldn't help myself.

The piano player, Al, made a face back at me.

Al is unusual. You can tell just by looking at him. He is thin and pale. His hair is so messy, I swear he never combs it. I once saw him zipping down Main Street on his bike. A woman walked in front of him, and he barked at her like a dog. She got out of the way fast!

I like Al. Sometimes he sticks his tongue out at Charlotte's back.

"What's the problem?" Al asked me. "Don't you

want to dance with Pat? I do! Come on, I'll switch places with you." Al started to get up from his piano bench. Then he flopped back down, looking disappointed. "I just remembered," he said. "I don't know how to dance."

Pat smiled at Al. "Come on," she urged me. "I promise not to step on your feet."

I knew Al and Pat were trying to make me feel better.

Pat's nice. I like having such a young ballet teacher. Pat even lets us call her by her first name. (Instead of making us call her Ms. Kelly.)

Pat is pretty too. She has straight, shiny black hair, fair skin, and a freckly face.

The girls in Pat's class call themselves Pat's Pinks. That's because the Intermediate dancers in our school wear pink leotards to class. The school is called Madame Trikilnova's Classical Ballet School.

Pat's great. But I still didn't want to dance with the *teacher*.

I had no choice. I walked toward the front of the studio.

Megan gave me a sympathetic smile as I passed her. That made me feel worse. I didn't want the kids in Glory to feel sorry for me. I wanted them to be my friends.

Two

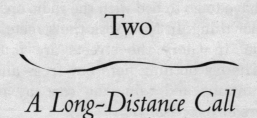

A Long-Distance Call

I hate it here, I told myself. *I absolutely, positively hate it*. The words *hate it* repeated in my head in time with my footsteps.

I walked by the coffee shop that is next door to the ballet school. Lots of the kids from the school hang out there after class. Nobody ever asked me to come. The only time I had been to the coffee shop was with my family.

I could see a group of Pat's Pinks inside. They were sitting at a window booth. They didn't seem to notice me even though I walked right by them. Just call me Invisible Jillian.

Sometimes I feel like an alien in Glory. An alien from New York City.

If you ask me, Glory is crazy. For one thing, it's too quiet. I'm used to the sounds of New York City: cars, motorcycles, garbage trucks, and

9

voices—*loud* voices. It's so quiet in Glory, I can't sleep. I have to go to bed with the radio on.

Another thing. In New York the streets are full of people. In Glory the streets are practically empty. There's nothing here but trees and birds and mountains and rain. You can say hello to every person you pass!

As I walked down Main Street, I searched for signs of life. I saw a woman hurry into the grocery store. Two old men were sitting on the bench in front of the bank. That was it. *Crazy,* I mumbled to myself.

A few minutes later I passed Charlotte's house. She lives down the street from my grandparents'. It's too bad none of the cool kids in Glory live on my street. Because one thing is certain. Charlotte and I are never going to be friends.

Charlotte acts as if she's better than everyone else. I admit that Charlotte dances well. But so do other kids in our class. Like Becky Hill. But you don't see Becky sticking *her* nose in the air.

Everyone around here seems to think Charlotte is pretty too. I guess she's okay-looking. Charlotte is tall and thin, with blond hair and blue eyes. But her clothes are *bor*-ing! She wears really average stuff: jeans, T-shirts, sweaters. That might not sound so bad. But *everything* she owns is pink, baby blue, or pale yellow. You're yawning, right?

Anyway, it's obvious Charlotte is a big deal in Glory. It's not that she's popular. It's more like the other girls are *afraid* of her. Not me. If Charlotte pushes me, I push her right back. I know how to handle her type.

The one thing I can't figure out about Charlotte is how she got Lynn Frazier to be her best friend.

Lynn smiles all the time. She's African-American, with dark skin and dark eyes. She wears her hair in cornrows. None of my friends from New York City would guess she was from a nowhere town in the Northwest. Lynn has lots of friends.

I turned up the walk to my grandparents' house. I gave the mailbox a little kick as I walked by it.

There are lots of things about my grandparents' house I like. There are also a lot of things I do *not* like. The mailbox was Number One on my do-not-like list.

The mailbox sits on a post near the sidewalk. The hand-painted lettering on its door reads, THE BELL RESIDENCE.

My grandparents are Mr. and Mrs. Bell.

My mom used to be Mrs. Kormach. But after the divorce, she changed her name back to Ms. Bell.

11

My last name is still Kormach. And "Kormach" is not on the mailbox. Like I said, just call me Invisible Jillian.

I opened the front door. I didn't even need to use my key. (My grandparents almost never lock the doors. I told you Glory was weird!)

The dogs rushed up to greet me.

"Hi, Darrow," I whispered, patting her on the head. "Shh, Marshall. Be quiet. I don't want Grandma to hear me."

Darrow and Marshall are weimaraners. That's a kind of dog with funky silver-gray fur.

Marshall loves Grandpa. But I'm Darrow's favorite.

The dogs are one great thing about living in Glory. Our apartment in Brooklyn is too small for a dog.

As soon as Marshall and Darrow quieted down, I tiptoed up the hallway. The dogs followed me. I stopped in front of my grandfather's study. I put my ear against the door and listened.

I didn't hear anything, so I opened the door and slipped inside. I let the dogs in, too. They flopped down on the rug. Quietly, I picked up the phone. I dialed a long-distance number. I was calling Maria Orsini. Maria is my best friend. She lives in my old neighborhood in Brooklyn.

Maria and I had been writing letters to each

other since I moved. I like to get letters, but it takes *so* long. Have you ever noticed that "mail" rhymes with "snail"?

I'm not allowed to make long-distance phone calls without permission. (My mom is super strict. I have to get permission for *everything*.) I did not have permission to call Maria. But I didn't care. I needed to talk to her. Besides, I knew my mother would say no if I asked.

The phone bill wouldn't come for a while. I would worry about breaking the rules then.

The Orsinis' phone rang four times.

I was about to hang up when Maria answered. "Orsini residence," she said, sounding all businesslike. I felt better just hearing her voice.

"Hi, Maria," I said.

"Hi, Jill!" Maria said. "Um, I mean, Jillian."

"You sound so far away," I told her.

Maria laughed. "I *am* far away. Something like three thousand miles. What time is it there?"

I glanced at the clock. "Five twenty-six," I said. "I just got home from ballet class."

"It's almost eight thirty here," Maria said. "I already ate dinner and finished my homework."

"That's so strange," I said. "I figured out that when I wake up, you've already been at school for more than an hour."

13

"I know," Maria said. "So how are things going there?"

"Terrible," I told her. "I hate it."

"Really?" Maria asked. "How come? You always loved to visit your grandparents."

"Living here is different," I said. "I miss my friends in New York. Especially since I don't have any in Glory."

"It can't be that bad," Maria said.

"It is," I insisted. Then I told Maria all about what happened in ballet class that afternoon.

"I can't believe nobody wanted to be your partner," Maria said when I finished.

"It's because they hate me," I said.

"They *can't*," Maria said. "Things will get better. The girls in Glory will realize how great you are soon."

I sighed. "If you say so. So what's new in the City?"

"Old Dillon is really being a meanie lately," Maria said. Mrs. Dillon is a teacher at the School of American Ballet. Maria is in her class. I used to be in it, too.

The School of American Ballet is another thing I miss about New York.

Everyone who loves ballet knows about the School of American Ballet. That's because hundreds of famous dancers have trained there. Nobody has ever heard of Madame Trikilnova's Classical Ballet School in Glory, Washington.

When I first started at the School of American Ballet, I was totally freaked out. Taking classes there was scary. But after a while, I stopped feeling afraid and started to feel special. I loved coming out of the school with my hair in a bun, carrying my black dance bag with toe shoes printed all over it. People walking down the street would look at me. I knew they were wondering if I was the next Darci Kistler.

I tried to tell Pat's Pinks about the School of American Ballet. But they weren't interested.

"I wish I were still taking ballet with you," I told Maria.

"Me too," Maria said. "It's not the same without you."

Just then I heard footsteps in the hallway.

Darrow stood up and let out a sharp bark.

"I have to go!" I whispered to Maria. I banged down the phone.

Three

Pad Thai

I yanked the dictionary out of the bookcase and opened it as quickly as I could. I pretended to be looking something up as my mother came into the room.

My mom is a lawyer. She had on a business suit and a bright-red silk blouse. She wears her hair in a short afro. Mom has incredible eyes—they're huge and coal-black. Everyone says I look just like her. I think they're crazy. Mom is much prettier than I am.

"Hi, Jill," Mom said. "How was your day?"

"Rotten," I said. "Nobody here wants to be friends with me. And my name is Jillian."

Back in New York, everyone called me Jill. When we moved here, I decided I wanted to be called Jillian instead. That's my real name. I think it's more glamorous than Jill.

16

Mom did not apologize for calling me the wrong name. "I have some business calls to make," she said. "Why don't you go help your grandmother with dinner?"

I slammed the dictionary down. I banged my way out of the study. I didn't like the way Mom had treated me. Sometimes I feel as if she doesn't care about me or my problems.

I walked into the kitchen. Instantly I started to feel happier.

"Something smells fabulous," I told my grandmother.

"Thank you," Grandma said, giving me a kiss on the cheek. "I hope you're hungry."

"Don't worry," I said. "If you're cooking, I'm hungry."

The kitchen counters were crowded with plates of cut-up veggies, shrimp, and tofu. A wok was on the stove. My mouth started to water.

I bet that when you hear "tofu," you think, Yuck! Who wants to eat bean curd? But you have to understand my grandma is a fabulous cook. She owns a restaurant in Seattle. It's called Hazel's. Hazel is Grandma's first name.

Grandma has long hair she wears up in a loose bun. It's gray in front, but the rest is still black. Grandma is light-skinned, like me.

17

Grandma has not worked in the restaurant since last summer. My aunt Christine started running the restaurant then.

Aunt Christine is great. She doesn't have any kids of her own. That means she loves to do things with me. We mostly do outdoor stuff together. Aunt Christine even promised to take me camping when the weather got warmer.

"What are you making?" I asked Grandma.

"Pad Thai," she said. "It's a dish from Thailand."

"I've had it before," I told her. "We ate lots of Thai food in New York. Dad loves it."

As soon as I mentioned Dad, I felt sad again. I couldn't help it. I missed him so much.

I still don't understand. Why did my parents have to get divorced?

My parents *never* fought. Even now they laugh when they talk on the phone.

Mom doesn't have a boyfriend. I wonder if Dad has a girlfriend. If he does, nobody has ever mentioned her to me. (Of course, that doesn't prove anything. Nobody ever tells me what's going on.)

My parents said they decided to get divorced because they weren't happy living together anymore. They said they had become different people with different interests. They each told me how much they loved me. They promised the divorce was not my fault.

About a week after my parents told me about the divorce, Mom and I moved into a new apartment. Dad stayed in our old place. I could go over and visit him anytime I wanted. I kept hoping Mom and Dad would change their minds and get back together.

But a few months later Mom told me we were moving to Glory. I didn't want to go. I didn't think it was right for Mom to take me so far away from Dad. I tried to talk Mom out of moving, but she wouldn't listen. Two weeks later all of our stuff had been boxed up.

Dad came to the airport to say good-bye.

"I want you to remember something," Dad told me while Mom and I waited to board the plane. "Even though we won't be seeing each other every day, I'm still your father."

I started to cry.

Dad started to cry.

I felt terrible. Mom and I were leaving Dad all alone. I cried for the entire flight.

I just don't understand. How could my parents let this happen? It makes me so angry. They should have tried harder to make each other happy.

"How was ballet today?" Grandma asked.

"It was okay," I told her. "But the school here is nothing like the School of American Ballet."

"You've told me that already," Grandma pointed out. "What did you learn today?"

"Nothing new," I said. "But we did a fun combination." (A combination is when you put a bunch of steps together into a minidance.)

"May I see it?" Grandma asked.

"Sure," I said.

I stepped out into the middle of the kitchen. I stood in fifth position. (My feet looked funny, since I was wearing tennis shoes instead of ballet slippers.) I did a *plié* (that's a knee-bend) and then a *relevé* to *demi-pointe* (that means I came up onto the balls of my feet). Then I fell sideways onto my right foot, bending my knee. That move is called a *tombé*. Next I did a *pas de bourrée* on *demi-pointe*. I crossed my left foot in back of my right one, brought my right foot to the side, then crossed my left foot in front of my right one. Left, right, left— that's an easy way to remember how to do a *pas de bourrée*. Then I jumped up and switched the position of my feet. That's called a *changement*.

"Ta da!" I said.

Grandma applauded. "Good job!"

"Thanks," I said.

Grandma turned back to the stove. She heated up the wok and poured in some oil. When the oil was hot, she threw the food in. It hit the wok with a sizzle.

Darrow and Marshall watched Grandma from their spot near the back door. Darrow licked her lips.

Grandma started to put the food onto serving dishes.

Suddenly Marshall jumped up. He ran toward the front door, barking and wagging his tail like mad.

"Grandpa is home," I said.

"Perfect timing," Grandma said.

Grandpa came into the kitchen. He kissed me and Grandma. Then he went to wash his hands for dinner.

My grandfather likes bow ties. He has a big collection. He was wearing a yellow one that day.

Grandpa is a lawyer, same as Mom and Dad. He has the only law office in Glory. It's downtown on Main Street. Now that we live here, Mom works with him. Grandpa is going to retire in a few years. When that happens, Mom is going to take over the office.

"Run and get your mother," Grandma told me. "Dinner is ready."

A few minutes later we all sat down and started to eat.

"This is yummy," I told Grandma.

Mom nodded.

"Thanks," Grandma said to me. "You know, I wouldn't mind if you invited friends over to dinner sometime."

I looked down at my plate. "I don't have any friends to invite," I said.

Nobody said anything for a minute.

Then Grandma reached over and patted my hand. "Don't worry," she said. "You'll make friends soon."

"The other girls will come around," Grandpa put in.

"Do you really think so?" I asked.

"I really do," Grandma said.

I studied my plate. I felt embarrassed. I was relieved when Grandpa changed the subject. For the rest of the meal we talked about the Mariners. That's the professional baseball team in Seattle.

"I'll help do the dishes," I announced when we were finished eating.

Mom stood up. "I can handle the dishes, Jill. You had better get started with your homework."

"My name is Jillian," I said.

"Okay, okay," Mom said. "Go do your homework, *Jillian*."

"Do I have to?" I asked.

Mom banged down the plate she was holding. "I don't want any more back talk from you," she practically screamed. "Now, do as I say."

I felt as if I was going to cry. Like I said, my mom has always been strict. But before the divorce, she never used to yell at me. I can't stand it when she yells.

I headed upstairs without saying another word. Darrow came with me. I sat down at my desk and opened my math book. Darrow sighed and curled up at my feet.

My room at my grandparents' amazes me. It is *so* big. I hung up my posters from Brooklyn, and the room still seems empty. I need to do some decorating, but I haven't felt like it yet.

I was looking at my first math problem when someone knocked on my door.

"Come in!" I yelled.

Grandpa opened the door. "I forgot to tell you earlier," he said. "I was in Seattle today and I bought you a book."

"Thanks!" I said. I love to read.

I took the book Grandpa was holding out.

It was *It's Not the End of the World* by Judy Blume. The book's back cover said the story was about a girl whose parents are getting divorced.

Grandpa sat down on my bed. "I know the divorce has been a big adjustment for you," he said.

"That's true," I told Grandpa.

"I thought this book might help," Grandpa said.

"Thanks," I said. "I'll start reading it as soon as I finish my homework."

"Good," Grandpa said.

I expected Grandpa to go, but he just kept sitting there. I smiled at him for a few seconds, but he didn't budge.

"Well . . ." I said. "I'd better start my math."

Grandpa cleared his throat. He looked uncomfortable. "Don't be angry with your mother," he blurted out. "She's going through a hard time. Things between you will get better soon."

"Okay," I said, looking down.

Grandpa left. I sat staring at my first math problem.

I could hear Mom and Grandma downstairs. They were talking and laughing. It was a happy sound. Mom and I used to laugh together, too. I wondered if we would ever do that again. It didn't seem possible.

Four

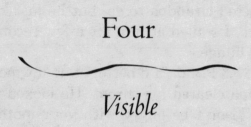

Visible

"Hello, Madame Trikilnova," I said with a big smile.

"Good afternoon, Miss Kormach," she said coldly.

As you probably guessed from the name of the ballet school, Madame Trikilnova owns it.

Madame Trikilnova always wears a black leotard and a flowing black skirt. She puts her blond hair into a neat bun every day. She's the type of person who looks perfect and expects you to do the same. What a drag.

I shook my head as I walked toward the dressing room.

Madame Trikilnova and I had gotten off to a bad start. Things between us have not improved since.

When I first signed up for ballet classes, I told Madame Trikilnova I belonged in an advanced class. I explained that I had studied at the School of American Ballet.

Madame Trikilnova was not impressed. "You must audition," she told me. "Then I will decide where you belong."

"Audition?" I asked. My stomach did a nervous flop. I had tried out for the School of American Ballet. But I never dreamed Madame Trikilnova would make me audition. I thought she would be thrilled to have a student from New York at her small-town school.

The audition did not go well. It's hard to dance when someone is watching you with angry eyes.

"You're not ready for an advanced class," Madame Trikilnova told me before I even finished performing the steps she requested. "You will be in Ms. Kelly's Intermediate One class."

"Intermediate One?" I asked. "Isn't that the easiest Intermediate class?"

"Yes," Madame Trikilnova said, turning away.

I ran after Madame Trikilnova as she strode down the hall. "I don't belong in Intermediate One," I argued. "I wasn't *that* bad."

"You will be in Intermediate One," Madame Trikilnova insisted. "If you belong in a higher level, you will be promoted."

I was furious. I was certain I would be bored in Intermediate I.

But I was wrong. My first class was great. It was also hard. I don't want to be promoted anymore.

Madame Trikilnova has been mean to me ever since that first day. She didn't like the way I bragged about the School of American Ballet. But *she's* just as bad. She's very proud that she danced with the Kirov. (That's a famous ballet company in Russia.) If Madame Trikilnova is so great, why isn't she running a school in a big city? I'd like her to explain that.

I pushed open the door of the dressing room.

Becky was coming out. "Hi," she said, hurrying by.

"Hi," I answered.

Becky disappeared into the stairway that leads up to the studio where we dance. Class did not start for twenty-five minutes. I don't understand how Becky gets ready so quickly. We get out of the same school at the same time. She must run all the way to the ballet school.

I went to my locker and started to change for class. Risa, Nikki, and Megan were already in the dressing room. They were talking as they put on their tights and leotards.

Becky, Nikki, Megan, Risa, and Katie are good friends. They're always together.

Risa is African-American. She wears her hair in

a bushy ponytail on top of her head. She has terrific green eyes and wears fairly cool clothes.

Katie has light-brown hair and brown eyes. She's smart and serious. She doesn't care much about what she wears.

Becky hasn't discovered clothes yet, either. The first thing you notice about her is her red hair.

Those five girls were the ones I liked best in Glory. I couldn't figure out why they didn't like me. I couldn't figure out why I was Invisible Jillian to them.

I listened to Risa, Megan, and Nikki talk as I pulled on my tights.

"What are you guys doing this weekend?" Risa asked the others.

Megan shrugged. "Nothing special."

"My parents are going on a trip," Nikki announced. "They leave tomorrow."

"Where are they going?" Risa asked.

"San Francisco," Nikki replied. "For a whole week."

"How come your parents aren't taking you?" Megan asked.

Nikki shrugged. "I don't know. But I don't mind staying home. My grandmother is coming to stay with me and Georgie."

Georgie is Nikki's little brother. Sometimes he

comes to the ballet school with Mrs. Norg to pick up Nikki.

"Your grandmother?" Risa asked. "I've never heard you talk about her."

"That's because she lives in Chicago," Nikki explained. "I don't see her much. But she always brings us great presents when she visits. Last time, she brought two frozen deep-dish pizzas. Everyone eats them in Chicago. They were yummy."

"I bet they weren't as good as New York pizza," I put in. "It's the best."

"Have you ever had Chicago pizza?" Nikki asked me.

"No," I said.

"Then you don't know what you're talking about," Nikki said. She turned to Megan and Risa. "Come on, you guys. Let's go."

The three of them left the dressing room together.

I felt very alone. I could not figure out why Pat's Pinks didn't want to be my friends.

The kids in Glory should have been impressed by me. I *am* from New York. I studied at the School of American Ballet. It didn't make sense that I wasn't super popular. Unless . . . everyone *was* impressed. Overwhelmed by my coolness. Scared of me!

That had to be it! And that meant all I had to do was give the other girls a break. I would approach them first. Pretty soon they would be fighting to spend time with me.

I hurried into the studio and took a place near Megan and Becky. I couldn't wait to put my plan into action.

"Hi, you guys," I said, trying to sound extra friendly. (I felt totally stupid.)

"Hey," Becky and Megan mumbled. They didn't even look up. Their attention was on the latest issue of *Dance Magazine*.

Dance Magazine comes out every month. It features articles on all different kinds of dance. Becky and Megan were examining the photographs.

I tried to think of something friendly to say. I peeked over Becky's shoulder and spotted an advertisement for toe shoes.

Ballerinas use toe shoes to dance on their toes. Pretty obvious, huh? Sometimes they're called pointe shoes, and dancing on your toes is called dancing on pointe.

If you don't study ballet, I bet you're wondering why anyone would want to dance on their toes. Sounds painful, right? It is painful. But it looks terrific. Every girl I know who takes ballet can't wait to dance on pointe. The problem is, you aren't supposed to start until you're eleven or twelve.

"Cool shoes," I said, pointing to the advertisement.

"I can't wait to start dancing on toe," Becky told me in a dreamy voice.

"I started toe in New York," I said. "It's great."

Becky and Megan looked up.

"Wow," Megan said.

"Really?" Becky asked. "Tell us about it!"

I bit my lip. Now that I had Megan and Becky's attention, I didn't want it. I had just told a huge lie. I had never danced on toe. I had never even tried on a pair of toe shoes. Like I said, I was much too young.

I wished I could take back the lie. But it was too late. Becky and Megan were waiting for me to tell them more.

Five

A Stupid Boast

"What was dancing on toe like?" Becky asked.

"Did you love it?" Megan said.

"Well—" I said.

"Becky," Pat called out. "Do you know where Katie is?"

Whew! Thank you, Pat!

"I haven't seen her today," Becky told Pat. "She's probably just late."

Pat frowned at her attendance sheet. "That's been happening too often lately," she mumbled.

Just then the studio door opened, and Katie slipped inside. Pat went over and whispered something in Katie's ear. Then she yelled, "Let's get started!"

"We'd better take our places," I told Becky and Megan.

"Okay," Becky agreed. "But will you tell us about dancing on toe later?"

"Sure," I said.

We each scrambled for a place at the barre. A barre is a handrail that runs along two or three sides of a ballet studio. Ballet classes always follow the same routine. First you do exercises to warm up your muscles. They're called barre exercises because you hold on to the barre while you do them. Center work comes next. During center work, you repeat a lot of the exercises you do at the barre—but you don't get to hold on. That makes them much harder. Traveling steps and jumps come last. That's the part of class when you do combinations.

All during the barre exercises that day, I could feel Megan and Becky watching me. We were doing *tendus*. I stretched my leg out from fifth position to fourth position in front, to second position to the side, and to fourth position in back. It's an easy move.

But remember how I told you ballet takes concentration? Well, I was not concentrating that day. I was worrying about my lie. My *tendus* were the worst. I kept bending my knees, and Pat kept reminding me not to.

"Let's move into the center," Pat told us when we finished all the barre exercise.

"Pat," Al spoke up. "I need a few minutes. I have a thumb cramp."

I was ninety-nine percent sure Al did *not* have a cramp in his thumb. He's always making stuff like that up.

"Take a five-minute break, kids," Pat said.

I groaned as Al headed for the studio door. How was I supposed to avoid Megan and Becky for five whole minutes?

Megan began to walk toward me. But before she got far, Dean started to talk to her. Yes!

I turned around to see where Becky was—and I almost smacked right into her! She had sneaked up behind me.

"How long did you take pointe?" Becky asked.

"I'm sorry," I said. "I—I have to go to the bathroom. I'll talk to you later."

I rushed out of the studio and hurried down to the dressing room. I locked myself into a bathroom stall. I counted to five hundred before I came out.

As I walked up the stairs, I could hear Al playing. Class had already started again. I ran the rest of the way to the studio and took my place.

Center work was just as bad as the barre. We were working on *développés*. In a *développé,* you bring one leg up until your toes touch your other knee. Then you straighten your leg out into the air. You do that to the front, side, and back. It takes a lot of balance and strength.

Développés are usually one of my favorite exercises. But I was still having a hard time concentrating. I kept losing my balance. And as soon as we finished in the center, Megan and Becky headed right for me.

I dashed up to Pat. "May I ask you a question?" I said.

"Sure," Pat said. "What's up?"

I had no idea what to ask. "Um—I have a cramp in my leg," I blurted out.

"You too?" Pat asked. "Cramps must be catching."

"Maybe I should go home," I suggested.

"No," Pat said. "Just rub it. Let me know if it starts bothering you more."

"Okay," I said. "When are we going to start traveling steps?"

"As soon as Al is ready," Pat said.

"Are you ready, Al?" I called to him.

"Yeah," he said.

"Al's ready," I told Pat. "We can start now."

Pat gave me a funny look. But she clapped her hands. "Places!" she called.

I hurried to a spot as far away from Becky and Megan as possible.

Pat showed us a combination. It was almost the same combination I had done for Grandma. The only difference was that Pat had taken out the *changement* and put in a *pirouette*. (*Pirouette* is ballet language for turn.)

The combination was not difficult. But I couldn't get the *pirouette* right. I had a hard time keeping my balance.

"Jillian, I want you to try that again," Pat said when everyone had taken a turn. "Megan and Dean, please dance with Jillian."

Megan, Dean, and I lined up. I was in the middle. Al began to play. The three of us started to dance. But with Megan right there, it was impossible to concentrate. I was worse than ever.

Pat frowned. She must have been surprised I was messing up such an easy combination. Nobody else was having a problem.

"Let's try this," Pat said. "Becky, come up front and demonstrate. Jillian, pay attention to Becky's feet. Watch her preparation. See how she makes a good strong turn?"

I watched Becky. But her demonstration did not help me. I was just too nervous to dance well. And *Becky* was half the reason I was nervous.

Pat had me do the combination again.

I messed up the *pirouette*. Again.

Pat patted me on the back. "Don't get frustrated," she said. "We'll try the combination again on Tuesday."

"Good," I told Pat. But the truth was, I didn't care about the *pirouette*. I was thinking that I had to tell Becky and Megan the truth. The sooner, the better.

I had been in this position before. Lying used to be a weird hobby of mine. It got me into a lot of trouble.

I had not lied in months. And I didn't want to start again. But I kept remembering how Megan and Becky snapped to attention when I told them I had started pointe work. After months of being Invisible Jillian, it had felt good.

"That's it, everyone," Pat called out. "Have a great weekend. I'll see you on Tuesday."

We all applauded for Pat and Al.

I made a break for the door.

"Hey, Jillian!" Becky called. "Wait up!"

Megan and Becky caught up to me before I got out of the studio.

"I can't believe you already started pointe," Becky said.

"I thought you had to wait until you were twelve," Megan added.

I stared at Becky and Megan. I imagined how disgusted they were going to look once they knew I had lied. Nobody likes to be lied to—I found that out the hard way. Becky and Megan would probably never talk to me again.

"How come you started so early?" Becky pressed.

I cleared my throat. It was time to confess. I opened my mouth—

"They start pointe earlier at the School of American Ballet," I said.

"But I thought starting too early damaged your feet," Megan said. "Aren't our bones supposed to be too soft or something?"

"The school X-rayed our feet before we started," I said. "My bones were hard enough."

"You're totally lucky," Becky said.

"It was pretty cool," I told her.

I know. You're wondering what happened to my confession. All I can say is, I couldn't help myself. I knew lying was bad. But not having any friends was worse. Besides, how would Becky and Megan ever find out what happened three thousand miles away?

"How long did you take pointe?" Becky asked.

"Almost a year," I told her.

"Was it hard?" Megan asked.

"At first," I said. "But after lots of practice, it gets easier."

"Did your toes bleed?" Megan asked.

"No way!" I said. "People just say that to gross you out."

"Did your ankles hurt?" Megan asked.

"A little," I said. "But it was worth it."

"Don't you miss it?" Becky asked.

"Tons," I said. "But sometimes I dance on toe at home. I don't want to forget everything I already learned."

Katie, Nikki, and Risa came back into the studio. They had already changed out of their leotards and tights.

"We were waiting for you," Nikki told Becky and Megan. "What are you doing up here?"

"Jillian is telling us about dancing on pointe," Becky explained.

"What does Jillian know about that?" Katie asked.

"A lot," Megan told her. "She danced on pointe in New York."

"Nobody starts pointe at nine," Katie said.

"Jillian did," Megan told her.

I smiled at Megan. I was happy she was standing up for me.

"If you studied pointe in New York, how come you aren't taking a pointe class here?" Risa asked.

"Well . . ." I said. "It's Madame Trikilnova. She won't let me. I don't think she likes me."

"Why not?" Becky asked.

I shrugged. "She thinks I'm a show-off."

"I agree!" Nikki said. "And I think you're just

showing off now. There's no way you started pointe."

"Give Jillian a break, you guys," Becky said. "You didn't even let her have a chance to prove it."

"How could she prove it?" Katie asked.

"She could bring her toe shoes to class," Megan suggested. "Right, Jillian?"

"No problem," I agreed.

Well, there was *one* problem. I didn't own a pair of toe shoes. But I wasn't about to say that.

Katie shook her head. "Having toe shoes doesn't prove anything. Anyone can buy a pair of toe shoes. There's only one way I'll believe Jillian took pointe."

"What's that?" Megan asked.

"I want to see her dance," Katie said.

Dance? In toe shoes? That was pretty funny. But how could I refuse? It would have been the same as admitting I was lying.

"I'll dance for you," I said. "It's no big deal."

"I'll believe it when I see it," Katie said. "Come on, you guys. Let's go."

Nikki and Risa followed Katie. But Megan and Becky hesitated.

"See you at school," Megan said.

"See you," I said.

"Bye, Jillian," Becky added.

41

"Bye," I replied.

After the others were gone, I walked down to the dressing room. All the other kids had left. Giselle, the ballet-school cat, rubbed up against my ankles while I stared into the mirror. I had two big problems:

(1) I didn't own toe shoes. (And I had no idea where to get a pair.)

(2) Even if I did find a pair of toe shoes, I didn't know how to dance in them.

I scooped up Giselle and buried my face in her fur.

"Mrrw," Giselle said.

"Help," I whispered back.

Six

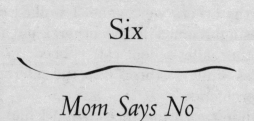

Mom Says No

"How was your day?" Mom asked me that evening as we were sitting down for dinner.

"It was okay," I told her.

"Don't you want to know about my day?" Mom asked me. "Say yes," she added in a loud whisper.

I grinned. "How was your day?" I asked, playing along.

"Great!" Mom said.

Grandpa put a serving dish down on the table. "What happened?" he asked.

"I ran into a friend from high school at the bank," Mom told him. "We spent almost an hour catching up."

Grandma came in with the bread basket. "It's always nice to see old friends," she said.

Mom nodded. "Guess what?" she said. "Helen has a daughter who's exactly Jillian's age."

"What's her name?" I asked.

"Becky Hill," Mom said.

"She's in my ballet class," I said. "And my class at school."

"I want to invite Helen over for dinner soon," Mom said.

"That's a good idea," Grandpa said.

"Becky could come, too," Mom told me.

The day before, I would have jumped for joy. But now everything was different. What if Becky told her mother I could dance on toe? Mrs. Hill might tell my mom.

"I think we should wait," I said.

"Why?" Mom asked.

"We have a big history project due at school," I said. "Becky and I will be very busy for the next few weeks."

Wow! I have no idea where *that* came from. Becky and I didn't have a history project due. Mr. Cosgrove, our teacher, had already finished our last history unit. School was going to be over in just two weeks. Once you start to lie, it's hard to stop.

"Okay," Mom agreed. "I guess there will be time for a dinner party this summer."

We cleaned our plates, and Grandma brought out a pecan pie.

Mom's eyes lit up. "My favorite dessert! You're spoiling me," she told Grandma.

Grandma grinned. "I'm just happy to have you here." She patted my hand. "Both of you."

I smiled. Everyone seemed to be enjoying themselves. It was the perfect time for me to pop my question.

"Mom?" I said. "Would you please buy me a pair of toe shoes?"

"Why do you want a pair of toe shoes?" Mom asked. "You're too young to dance in them."

"I just want them," I said. "I haven't asked for anything in a long time."

"I'll be happy to buy you a pair of toe shoes," Mom said.

"Thanks—" I started.

"Wait," Mom interrupted. "You didn't let me finish. I'll be happy to buy you a pair *when* your class starts doing pointe work in a few years."

"Couldn't we get them now?" I asked. "I'll take good care of them until I start pointe."

"No," Mom said. "Who knows what size your feet will be in a few years? Toe shoes are expensive. I don't want to waste money buying a pair in the wrong size."

Grandma started to say something. But Grandpa waved his hand at her. Grandpa thinks

Mom should be allowed to raise me her own way. He doesn't want Grandma to interfere.

"We're not poor, you know," I said hotly.

"No, we're not," Mom agreed.

"You like to act like we are!" I yelled.

"That's enough, Jillian," Mom said.

When my mother says "that's enough," she means it. I knew better than to argue. But I couldn't help it. I was angry.

"You don't care about what I want," I yelled at Mom. "You have eighteen pairs of shoes you never wear. But I can't have one pair I really want."

Mom put down her fork and gave me her full attention. "Go to your room," she said. "I don't want to see you until morning."

"But she hasn't finished her pie," Grandma said.

"Then she'll have to live without it," Mom said.

"You wouldn't care if I starved!" I screamed at her.

I ran upstairs. I slammed my bedroom door as hard as I could. I threw myself down on my bed and had a long cry.

Then I fell asleep.

It was dark when I woke up. My clock said 7:35. I had been asleep for about thirty minutes. I still had almost an hour before bedtime.

I did my homework and finished another couple of chapters of *It's Not the End of the World*. I decided to ask Grandma for a piece of pecan pie at breakfast.

Around bedtime Grandma knocked on my door. "Phone for you," she told me. "Hurry up. It's long distance."

I jumped up and ran for the phone. "Hello?" I said.

"Hey, Jillian!"

It was my dad! (Unlike *some* people, he didn't have any trouble remembering I didn't want to be called Jill anymore.)

"Hi, Daddy!" I yelled.

Dad calls me once a week. I'm always happy to hear from him. Sometimes I worry that he might forget about me.

"How are you?" Dad asked.

My throat got all choked up. "I'm okay," I whispered. "But I miss you a lot."

"I miss you, too," Dad said. "Tell me all about what you've been doing."

I told Dad about what Mr. Cosgrove taught us that week. Then I told him the latest on Madame Trikilnova and her grudge against me.

Dad told me about a big case he was working on.

We talked until Dad and I both started yawning. It was past *both* our bedtimes. (It was after midnight in New York.) Before Dad hung up, he asked if I needed anything.

"Yes," I said right away. "I need a pair of toe shoes. I wear a size two in regular shoes."

Asking Dad for toe shoes was kind of silly. Mom always takes me to buy tights and leotards and stuff like that. Dad doesn't know a *pirouette* from a parrot. He never buys me anything for dance class.

"I don't know, kiddo," Dad said. "I like to let your mother deal with your ballet gear."

"I know," I whispered. "That's okay."

After I got off the phone, I lay awake in bed. I had to come up with a way to get a pair of toe shoes. Before I fell asleep, I thought of one person who could help me.

Seven

Maria Says No

"How is everything, folks?" Mr. Stellar asked.

"Great," Grandma told him.

It was Saturday morning. Outside it was warm and clear. My family was eating a late breakfast at the coffee shop on Main Street. It's next to the ballet school, remember? The little restaurant was crowded.

Mr. Stellar poured more coffee for the grown-ups. I sighed. I felt as if we had been sitting there forever. I had something important to do that morning—*if* we ever got home. I had to get back into Grandpa's study. Alone. I wasn't quite sure how I was going to do it.

Dean and Philip—the twins from my ballet class—were rushing around. The twins' parents own the coffee shop. Dean was cleaning tables. Philip was doing dishes.

Philip and Dean are twins, but they don't look or act anything like each other. Philip has dark-brown hair and eyes. He is short. He loves football and hates ballet.

I don't know how Dean feels about football, but he loves ballet. Dean is taller and thinner than his brother. He has light-brown curly hair and blue eyes.

"Hi," I said to Dean when he came over to clear our table.

"Hi," Dean said. "I've heard a lot about you lately."

"Really?" I said. "What have you heard?"

Oops! I suddenly knew Dean was about to say someone told him I could dance on pointe. I also realized my mother and grandparents had stopped talking. They were waiting to hear what Dean was going to say. I had to do something—*fast*.

"Wait," I said to Dean in a teasing tone. "Did *Megan* tell you?"

Dean was balancing a pan full of dirty dishes on the edge of our table. "Um, yeah," he said.

"You like her a lot, don't you?" I asked.

Dean's face turned bright red.

My mom and grandparents were really paying attention now.

"She's nice," Dean said.

"I know *that*," I said. "I was asking if you liked her as a *girlfriend*."

Dean lost control of the dish pan. It fell to the floor with a huge crash. Dirty dishes slid under our table.

Grandma gasped.

Everyone in the restaurant turned to stare. Mrs. Stellar hurried over and started to apologize.

"Don't worry," Grandpa said. "Dean just got a little flustered."

Philip came out of the kitchen with a mop.

"We'll get out of your way," Mom said, putting some money on the table.

A minute later my family was out on the sidewalk. We started to walk home. Grandma gave me a funny look. "I do believe you were teasing that Stellar boy," she said.

"Maybe," I admitted.

"I thought you were too young to like boys," Mom said.

"I don't like boys," I said. "But Dean likes Megan."

"Lovely day," Grandpa said loudly. (He always knows when to change the subject.) "It'll be time to put in the garden soon."

Mom's eyes lit up. "I'll help with the tomatoes," she told Grandpa. Mom turned to me.

"Wait until you taste them, Jill. Nothing is more delicious than homegrown tomatoes."

"I remember when you and Christine were kids," Grandma told Mom. "The two of you used to eat the tomatoes right off the vine. You ate them standing up in the garden."

"We can decide where to put the plot when we get back to the house," Grandpa suggested.

When we got home, the adults wandered toward the garden. They didn't even go inside first.

Mom held her hand out to me. "Come on, honey," she said.

"I'll be out later," I said.

Mom dropped her hand. "Okay," she said, looking disappointed.

Mom walked around the side of the house. I let myself inside and hurried down the hall to Grandpa's study. I dialed Maria's number. Just in case Maria's mom or dad answered, I got ready to hang up.

"Hello?"

"Maria!" I said. "Hi. It's me, Jillian."

"Hey," Maria said. "Aren't you going to get in trouble for calling me so much?"

"Probably," I told her. "But I need your help."

"What's up?" Maria asked.

"I want you to get me a pair of toe shoes," I told her.

"Toe shoes?" Maria repeated. "How come?"

I told Maria about Becky and Megan and how I told them I could dance on pointe. Then I told her about Katie and Nikki and Risa and how they thought I was lying.

"Well, you are lying," Maria reminded me.

"I know," I said. "Anyway, can you help me get the shoes?"

"No," Maria said.

"Why not?" I asked.

"Because you're never going to make friends by telling lies," Maria said.

"Maria," I said in a warning tone. "I don't want a lecture."

"I just don't want you to get in trouble," Maria said. "Things always get out of hand when you start lying."

"That's not true," I said.

"It is so," Maria insisted. "Remember the time you told everyone at school that Neneh Cherry was your cousin?"

In case you don't know, Neneh Cherry is one of the best singers in the world. All the kids at my old school love her.

"Yeah," I said. "So?"

"When everyone found out you were lying, the entire school was mad at you," Maria said.

"Nobody—except for me—talked to you for weeks. You were miserable."

"This is different," I said.

"How?" Maria asked.

"Nobody in Glory talks to me anyway," I told her.

"Lying won't help you make friends," Maria insisted.

"You have to get the shoes for me," I told Maria. "What will I tell Becky and Megan if you don't?"

"Tell them the truth," Maria said firmly.

Maria is incredibly stubborn. It's stupid to fight with her once she makes up her mind.

"I have to go," I said. I was furious. Maria is such a goody-goody. She makes me sick sometimes.

"I'm trying to help," Maria told me.

"Bye!" I yelled. I hung up the phone before Maria could say anything more.

I couldn't think of anyone else who could get the toe shoes for me. It was just a matter of time before everyone discovered I was lying.

Eight

An Invitation

"You look glamorous," I told Nikki.

"Do you think so?" Nikki asked.

"Definitely," I told her.

Becky and Megan nodded.

It was four days later. I was eating lunch with Nikki, Megan, and Becky. I had been spending more time with them at school. (Katie and Risa go to private school. That's why they weren't around.)

I was starting to feel comfortable with Becky and Megan. But things between Nikki and me were strange. Some days—like the day I had promised to dance on pointe—I couldn't stand Nikki. Other days, I thought she was great.

Nikki seemed to feel the same way about me. Sometimes she was a real snot. Other times, she acted like my best friend. That day, Nikki and I were getting along. Everyone was in a happy

56

mood. School was almost out! Summer vacation would start in one week.

I had been going to Glory Elementary for about three months. It felt more like three years. I had eaten lunch by myself almost every one of those days. Sitting in the lunchroom alone is *so* embarrassing.

Eating with the other girls was a big improvement. But I couldn't enjoy it. I still hadn't told the others I had lied about starting pointe.

I was beginning to think they had forgotten about my promise. Nobody had mentioned toe shoes for days. I wasn't about to bring up the subject. I was convinced that when the others learned the truth, they wouldn't want to be my friends.

Besides, nobody was interested in a confession at that moment. Everyone was busy talking about Nikki's hair.

"Why did you decide to cut it?" Megan asked.

"It was Jillian's idea," Nikki said.

I almost choked on my sandwich. "What?" I coughed out.

"Remember in ballet the other day?" Nikki asked me. "I was complaining about my hair—"

"And I told you to cut it!" I finished for her.

Nikki nodded. "I thought it was a great idea," she said. "But I was scared. Then yesterday Grandma took me and Georgie to Seattle. We walked by a hair salon. I got up my nerve and asked Grandma if I could get my hair cut. She said yes right away."

"She did?" Megan asked.

Nikki nodded. "Grandma had just spent an hour trying to brush a knot out of my hair," she explained.

"You're not going to get any more knots," Becky told Nikki.

We all laughed. Nikki's hair was now about an inch long all over. She looked terrific. You could even see her eyes. It was a two-hundred-percent improvement.

"Guess what?" Becky said. "I'm having a party on Saturday. If it's warm enough, we're going to barbecue."

"What's the party for?" Megan asked.

Becky turned a little pink. "It's for Katie."

"Is it her birthday?" I asked.

"No," Becky said. "I just owe her."

Nikki giggled.

I gave Becky a puzzled look. "Why do you owe her?"

"It's a long story," Becky mumbled.

"Katie threw a party for Becky a few months ago," Megan explained. "But because they had a fight, Becky didn't show up."

"You and Katie seem like such good friends," I told Becky. "I can't imagine you fighting."

"It wasn't all Becky's fault," Megan said. "Charlotte Stype helped."

I made a face. "That girl is trouble."

"You said it!" Nikki exclaimed.

"Do you guys want to come to my party or what?" Becky asked.

"Definitely," Nikki said.

"I'll be there," Megan added.

I did not say anything. I wasn't sure Becky had meant to include me.

"Jillian?" Becky asked. "Will you come?"

"Sure," I said. I wanted to act cool. But I couldn't stop smiling. I was psyched. It was the first invitation I had received since moving to Glory.

The bell rang. We stood up and gathered our stuff together.

"See you," Nikki said. She ran to catch up with Kim, who is in her class.

"Dean and I decided to buy Mr. Cosgrove a gift for the last day of school," Megan said to me and Becky as we walked down the hall toward our classroom. "It's going to be from the whole class."

Becky and I exchanged surprised glances.

"If you want to contribute, you can give money

to Dean or me," Megan added. She walked ahead of us into the classroom.

"This is getting serious," Becky told me in a whisper. "Dean and Megan are making secret plans together."

I shook my head. "Boy craziness," I said. "It's a disease."

Nine

Pointe Class

"Jillian!" Becky called the next afternoon.

I looked down the second-floor hallway of the ballet school. Becky, Megan, Katie, Nikki, and Risa were crowded around Studio D's doorway. Our class is held in Studio C.

"What are you guys doing?" I called.

Becky motioned to me. "Come here!"

"Class is starting," I whispered as I walked up to Becky.

"I don't care if we're late," she whispered back.

"You don't care?" I repeated. "Something really interesting must be going on."

"It is," Megan whispered. "Look!"

I peeked over Becky's shoulder. Inside the studio, Madame Trikilnova was teaching an advanced pointe class.

"Watch the girl with the black headband,"

Becky whispered. "She's the best."

"Her name is Heather McCabe," Katie added.

Heather was the tallest girl in her class. Lots of tall kids are clumsy, but Heather moved with grace. She was thin, with powerful-looking arms and legs.

The girls were doing a complicated combination. I didn't even know the names of half the steps.

"Can you do that?" Megan asked me. "On pointe, I mean."

I laughed. "The combination? No way! But I can do a *relevé,*" I said, naming one of the easiest moves the older girls were performing.

"What else can you do?" Katie asked.

"Um—" I studied the combination for another easy move. "*Bourrées.*"

"*Bourrées* look terrific on pointe," Becky said.

"Can you do an *arabesque*?" Risa asked. In an *arabesque* you support your weight on one foot and hold the other leg up behind you. There are lots of different kinds.

"Sure," I said. The older girls were doing *arabesques* as part of their combination. But I figured I could do one holding on to the barre. That couldn't be too hard.

I noticed Katie studying my face. I realized all

the moves I had mentioned were easy. If I wanted the others to believe I had studied pointe, I had to say I could do something more difficult.

"I can also do a *pirouette,*" I said.

Becky looked surprised. "You really had a hard time with the *pirouettes* in class last week," she said.

I shrugged. "I was having a bad day."

"But—" Becky started.

I gasped.

"What happened?" Becky asked.

"One of the girls almost fell," I lied.

"Really?" Becky asked. "Which one?"

"The one with curly black hair," I said, pointing.

"I didn't see her fall," Katie said.

"I didn't *say* she fell," I told her. "I said she *almost* fell."

Becky did not argue with me about *pirouettes* after that. She was too busy watching the dancers. She didn't want to miss anything interesting.

"Hello," a voice said.

I turned around. Pat was standing behind us. "Did you guys forget something?" she asked.

"We're sorry we're late," Becky said. But she didn't move from her spot by the door. She didn't even turn around.

"Can we watch for a little longer?" Risa asked.

"The rest of the class is waiting," Pat pointed out.

"Please," Megan and Katie said together.

Pat smiled. "All right," she said. "You can watch until Madame Trikilnova gives her girls a break. But then come straight to class."

"We will," we all promised.

Pat headed back down the hall to Studio C. Things got quiet. Becky, Megan, Risa, Nikki, and Katie were watching the older girls closely. I was happy to be included.

A few minutes later Madame Trikilnova gave her class a break.

"I guess we have to go to class now," Megan said sadly.

"I don't mind," Becky said. "I'm ready to dance. I want to practice. Otherwise, I'll never get up on pointe."

As we were turning toward Studio C, Madame Trikilnova came out into the hallway. She took one look at Nikki and gasped.

"Miss Norg!" Madame Trikilnova exclaimed. "What happened to your hair?"

"I got it cut," Nikki said.

"How silly!" Madame Trikilnova said. "You must grow it out at once!"

"How come?" Nikki asked.

"Everyone knows that you can't dance ballet with short hair," Madame Trikilnova said. "It goes against tradition."

Nikki had a funny look on her face. She didn't say anything.

"That's stupid," I told Madame Trikilnova. "Baryshnikov doesn't have long hair."

Megan covered her mouth so that Madame Trikilnova wouldn't hear her giggle.

Katie was grinning.

Madame Trikilnova turned to face me. "Baryshnikov is a man, not a young girl," she told me. "Besides, I don't see how this concerns you."

Madame Trikilnova stormed down the hall.

I stuck my tongue out at her back.

Becky gave me a horrified look.

Megan pulled on my hand. "Come on," she said. "We have to get to class."

Pat smiled at us as we pushed open the door to Studio C.

The class was doing stretches on the floor. Pat hadn't started the barre exercises yet. She was waiting for us.

"Did you guys see anything interesting?" Pat asked.

"It was all interesting," Becky told her. "I can't wait to start pointe. It's beautiful."

"No fair," Charlotte said with a pout. "I didn't get to watch."

I grinned at Charlotte. I was glad she had been left out.

"I tell you what," Pat said. "I'll arrange a pointe demonstration for the whole class."

Charlotte smiled smugly. "That sounds great."

"We have some time to make up," Pat said. "Let's get started."

Everyone scrambled for a place at the barre.

I ended up standing next to Megan.

"Don't forget to bring your toe shoes in," Megan whispered as we dropped into our first *plié*.

"I won't," I whispered back.

The others had forgotten about my promise for a while. But watching the older girls dance had reminded them. Not only that, I had told them I could do a *pirouette*. How was I going to get out of this mess now?

Ten

Grounded

"Hi, Darrow," I said. "Hi, Marshall."

Darrow jumped up and licked my face.

Marshall was going nuts. He couldn't wag his tail fast enough.

I giggled.

Dogs are easy. They don't judge you the way people do. You feed them and they love you.

People are tough. The harder I tried to make them like me, the more lies I told. I wanted to stop. But how?

Suddenly I knew what to do. I had to tell Mom everything. She would help me set things right.

"Jillian!" Mom yelled. "Is that you?"

"Yes!" I cried.

Mom was home from work early! We could talk right away.

"Would you come in here a second?" Mom called.

"Coming!" I yelled, hurrying toward the dining room.

Mom was sitting at the dining room table. She was surrounded by bills.

"Hi," I said, giving Mom a kiss.

"Hi, honey," Mom said. "How was your day?"

I shrugged. "The usual," I said. "Can we talk about something? It's important."

"Sure," Mom said. "But I want you to look at this first." She sorted through the piles of paper in front of her. After a few seconds she found what she was looking for: the phone bill.

"Did you make these calls to New York?" Mom asked.

My heart dropped down to my knees.

"No," I said. That was *another* lie. I knew the charges were for the calls I made to Maria.

Mom held the bill out to me. "Take a look," she said. "Don't you recognize the number?"

I took the bill and pretended to study it. "No," I said.

"That's funny," Mom said. "It belongs to your best friend."

"Okay," I said. "I admit it. I called Maria."

"Twice," Mom said.

"Twice," I agreed.

"I was going to let this slide," Mom said. "But I don't like the way you just lied to me."

I didn't say anything.

"Jill, you promised to give up lying," Mom reminded me.

"You promised to give up calling me Jill!" I yelled.

Mom frowned.

"I did give it up," I whispered.

"You gave it up?" Mom asked, raising her eyebrows. "Then why did you lie to me just now?"

"I don't know," I whispered.

"You know what this reminds me of—" Mom started.

"Mom!" I shouted. "Don't!"

I knew just what my mom was about to say. I hate it when she brings up things I did months ago. It's totally unfair. Why can't she just forgive and forget?

You're dying to know what she was going to say, aren't you? Okay, here's the story:

Last fall, back before my parents got divorced, there was this movie I really wanted to see. It was called *Slayer, Part 6*. It was rated R.

A girl in my class—her name is Jamie—asked me to see the movie with her family. I definitely wanted to go.

69

The problem was, my parents thought I was way too young to see R movies. Sometimes they treat me like a baby. But that doesn't mean I have to act like one.

That Friday evening, I told my parents I was going to Maria's. Then I went to the movies with Jamie and her family.

Everything was cool. Then my mother called Maria's. I have no idea why—but she called.

Maria's mom told her I wasn't there. Mom freaked. She called Dad at his office. (He was working late.) Dad freaked. Mom and Dad rushed over to Maria's house. My parents and Maria's parents ganged up on Maria until she told them where I was.

Meanwhile, Jamie's parents had dropped me off at home. I was wondering where Mom and Dad were when they stormed in.

Dad calmed down fast. But, boy, was Mom mad! I got into huge trouble. I promised Mom and Dad that I would never, ever lie again. And I haven't lied since. Well, not until this week.

(By the way, I also had nightmares for a month. That movie was *really* scary.)

Mom took the phone bill back. "I don't want your lying to get out of hand," she told me.

"It won't," I said.

"I think you could use some time to think about what you did," Mom said.

I knew what was coming. "You can't ground me," I said.

"I can and I will," Mom said. "You're grounded for the weekend. No TV, no phone. I want you home all day Saturday and Sunday."

"But, Mom," I said. "Becky's barbecue is on Saturday."

"You'll have to cancel," Mom told me.

"I can't cancel!" I yelled. I took a deep breath and tried to calm down. I had to make Mom understand.

"The kids in Glory have ignored me for months," I told her. "Becky is the first one to include me. You have to let me go!"

"No," Mom said.

"This isn't fair!" I said. "You're so mean!"

"I'm not discussing this any further," Mom told me. "Now, please go to your room."

I stared at Mom for a long moment. I couldn't believe I had been about to ask her for help. She wouldn't have helped me. She didn't care about my problems.

All the anger I was holding inside spilled out.

"I hate you!" I yelled as loudly as I could. "I hate you!"

Eleven

Nikki's Grounded

"I brought some money for Mr. Cosgrove's present," Becky told Megan Friday morning at school. She took a rumpled dollar out of her pocket and gave it to Megan.

"Me too," I said, putting a handful of change down on Megan's desk.

Megan smoothed out Becky's dollar. Then she took an envelope out of her desk. She put our money inside.

"Almost everyone in the class has contributed," Megan reported. "Dean and I are going to pick out a present tomorrow morning. I'll show you what we bought at the barbecue."

"I won't be there," I said. "I'm grounded."

"How come?" Becky asked.

"My mom is mad because I—" I stopped. I couldn't say Mom grounded me for lying. If I did,

Megan and Becky might guess I was lying about pointe too.

"My mom is mad because I didn't do well on our last spelling test," I said.

"I'm a great speller," Becky said. "I can help you if you want."

I'm a great speller, too. I imagined myself going over to Becky's and pretending to be a bad one. That would be hard to pull off.

"No, thanks," I said. "My mom doesn't like me to study with other people."

"Why not?" Megan asked.

"She thinks it's just an excuse to play," I said.

"Your mother sure is strict," Megan said.

"I know," I said. "I hate it."

"My barbecue isn't going to be much fun," Becky said. "Hardly anyone can come. Nikki is grounded, too."

"What happened?" I asked.

"Her parents came home yesterday," Megan said. "Mrs. Norg freaked out about Nikki's hair. She grounded her *forever*."

"But Nikki's hair looks great," I said. "Besides, she didn't sneak out and get it cut, or anything like that. Her grandmother took her."

"Yeah, but Nikki's *mother* wouldn't have let her cut her hair in a million years," Megan said.

"Why not?" I asked.

"Because Mrs. Norg is a real wacko," Becky told me.

"A wacko?" I asked.

Megan sighed. "Mrs. Norg wants Nikki to be famous," she explained. "Nikki only takes ballet lessons because her mother makes her."

"Nikki also takes drama lessons in Seattle," Becky added. "Plus, Mrs. Norg makes her audition for plays. And she signed her up with a modeling agency."

"What's wrong with that?" I asked. "It sounds like fun."

"I think so, too," Becky said. "But Nikki hates it."

"Sometimes it is kind of yucky," Megan said.

"Remember the movie?" Becky asked her.

Megan nodded. "A TV movie was being shot in Seattle last year," she explained. "They needed a bunch of girls to be extras. A bunch of *five-year-old* girls."

Becky took up the story. "Mrs. Norg didn't care that Nikki was eight. She made her wear a frilly dress and put her hair into pigtails. Nikki really did look about five years old by the time Mrs. Norg finished with her."

"That sounds terrible," I said.

"You haven't heard the worst part yet," Megan told me.

"Nikki got a part!" Becky exclaimed. "She had to spend an entire weekend hanging out with babies!"

"Poor Nikki!" I said.

I was still miserable. But I felt a little better, thanks to Megan and Becky. My mother may be the strictest mother in the United States. But Mrs. Norg sounded even worse.

Twelve

Thanks, Dad

"Jillian!" Mom yelled. "Come down here, please!"

"Now what?" I mumbled.

It was Saturday. I had spent the entire morning thinking about the fun I should have been having at Becky's barbecue. I was furious with my mother for grounding me. I hadn't apologized for saying I hated her—and I wasn't about to.

I stomped downstairs. "What do you want?" I asked.

"The mail came," Mom told me. "I thought you might be interested in this."

She held up a box.

I grabbed it from her. The postmark was from Brooklyn. Our old address was written on the left-hand corner. I recognized the handwriting.

"It's from Dad!" I shouted.

"I know," Mom said. "Let's see what it is."

I ripped open the package. I couldn't believe what was inside. It was a pair of toe shoes!

Mom peeked into the box. "What a strange gift," she said.

"It's a *great* gift," I said.

"Well, I don't want you messing around with those," Mom said. "You could hurt yourself."

I just rolled my eyes.

"I'll take care of the package for you," Mom said. She held out her hand. She kept it out until I gave her the box.

Can you believe that? She didn't even trust me to keep the toe shoes myself.

I stormed into the living room. Grandpa was sitting in his favorite chair, reading a fat law book.

"That looks boring," I told him.

"It's not," Grandpa said. "But it is kind of heavy. My arms are getting tired."

I couldn't help but smile.

"How's the book I gave you?" Grandpa asked me.

"I finished it this morning," I said. "It was good."

"Tell me about it," Grandpa suggested.

"The main character's name is Karen," I said. "Her parents get divorced just like Mom and Dad did. Except that Karen is luckier than I am. She gets to see her father all the time."

Grandpa motioned for me to come closer.

I went and stood in front of his chair.

Grandpa put his hands on my shoulders and looked me in the eye. "You're going to see your dad this summer," he reminded me. "But that's not the important thing. The important thing is that you know your mom and dad love you just as much now as they did before the divorce."

"Mom doesn't love me," I said.

Grandpa gave my shoulders a tiny shake. "Yes, she does," he said.

Then Grandpa did a funny thing. He started to laugh!

"Of course, your mom *is* mighty strict," he said. "Almost as strict as I was when she was a little girl."

"You were strict with Mom?" I asked.

"Absolutely," Grandpa said.

"If I ever have a little girl, I'm going to be the nicest mother in the whole world," I announced.

Grandpa really laughed at that! "We'll see," he said. "Now, let me get back to my reading. I have to finish this book."

I went upstairs. I had just started to write a letter to Maria when Mom poked her head into my room.

"I'm going out," Mom said. "See you later."

"Where are you going?" I demanded.

"To a movie with Helen," Mom said.

Helen? That was Becky's mother. I didn't like the idea of Mom going out with her. Becky might have told her mother about my promise.

"What about me?" I asked.

"Your grandparents are going to stay with you," Mom said.

"How come you get to go out when I'm stuck here?" I asked angrily. "That's not fair."

"You're grounded," Mom reminded me. "I'm not."

If you ask me, Mom was not being very nice. She had already grounded me. She didn't have to rub it in. I felt like doing something to get back at her.

I decided to dance in my new toe shoes.

As soon as Mom was gone, I went into her bedroom. I found the box from my father in her closet. I took it into my room and sat down on my bed. I opened the box and lifted out the shoes. Underneath I found a note from Dad. This is what it said:

Dear Jillian,

These are the smallest toe shoes made. I hope they aren't too big. The saleswoman suggests putting lamb's wool in the toes. Enjoy!

Love,
Daddy

I put the note back in the box, took off one of my

tennis shoes, and tried on one of the toe shoes. I could barely point my foot with it on. Then I remembered that the dancers at the School of American Ballet bent back their new toe shoes before they wore them. Carefully I bent one shoe and then the other. That softened them up a little.

I still had a problem. I needed ribbons to hold the shoes on. There weren't any ribbons attached. But I wasn't worried. All I had to do was sew some on.

I put the shoes back into their box and hid them under my bed. Then I ran downstairs. I found Grandma in the backyard. She was on her hands and knees, clearing ground for the garden. "May I borrow a needle and thread?" I asked her.

"Sure," Grandma said, sitting back on her heels. "Look in the junk drawer in the kitchen."

I ran back toward the house.

"What are you sewing?" Grandma called after me. "Do you need help?"

I stopped running and spun around to face her. "No!" I yelled. "I'm just, um, fixing a hole in one of my leotards."

Another lie.

"Okay," Grandma said, turning back to her work. I ran inside before Grandma could ask any more questions. I got the needle and thread, and hurried back up to my room.

I had lots of hair ribbons in the top drawer of my dresser. I moved things around until I found two that weren't too wrinkly. Unfortunately, they were different colors. I decided one shoe would have white ribbons. The other would have pink. Usually the ribbons on toe shoes match, but what could I do?

I pricked myself with the needle about a hundred times before I finally got the ribbons to stay on.

When I tied the shoes on, they seemed big. Then I remembered Dad's note. I ran down the hall to my mom's bathroom. There wasn't any lamb's wool in the medicine cabinet. I grabbed a handful of cotton balls instead.

I went back to my room, put the cotton balls in the shoes, and ran up to the attic.

The attic door does not have a lock. I put a big chair in front of it. I didn't want anyone to walk in on me.

I put the toe shoes on and carefully stood up. My feet felt huge and wooden.

Holding on to a chair, I tried a *relevé*.

When you're dancing in regular ballet slippers, *relevés* are no big deal. All you have to do is raise your heels off the floor. You support your weight on the balls of your feet. On pointe it's not so easy. I had to lift up my heels, the balls of my feet, and support myself on the tips of my toes. Ouch! My toes did not like that.

My ankles and knees wobbled. I had to try many times before I could do a *relevé*. Then I tried letting go of the chair. I fell. It was fifteen minutes later when I finally did a *relevé* without holding on.

By that time I had more confidence. I did another *relevé* without any problem. Then I held on to the chair and tried an *arabesque*. Then *bourrées*.

Dancing on pointe was fun. I forgot to worry about the other girls. I forgot to feel angry at my mother. My toes hurt whenever I stopped, but when I was dancing I felt wonderful.

I decided to try a *pirouette*. I took a deep breath, prepared, and pushed off. But I never made it onto pointe. It was even harder than I imagined to *pirouette* with toe shoes on. But I wasn't about to give up. I tried again and again—for a whole half hour—until I finally got up on pointe.

The time after that, I made it halfway around before I fell. The next two times, I did complete *pirouettes*. But they were both shaky. Keeping my balance on the toes of one foot was incredibly difficult.

My legs were becoming wobbly.

I decided I had practiced enough for one day. Mom would probably be back any minute. I put the toe shoes in their box and put the box in Mom's closet. As long as she didn't take the box down and see that the shoes had ribbons attached, everything would be fine.

I lay down on my bed and thought about my afternoon's practice. I was almost positive I could do a perfect *pirouette* when my legs weren't tired.

If I did a *pirouette* on pointe, Megan, Becky, Nikki, Risa, and Katie would believe I had been telling the truth. They would want to be my friends.

I promised myself that once I had friends in Glory, I would never lie again. Lying is scary. And this lie was the scariest one I had ever told. If I didn't pull it off, I would be an outcast forever.

Thirteen

Class Visitor

"Did you get your hair caught in a fan or something?" Charlotte asked Nikki before ballet.

"You're not even funny," Nikki told her.

"What did you say?" Charlotte asked. "It wasn't a fan? It was a lawn mower. Well, that explains it."

Nikki just rolled her eyes. She seemed to have run out of nasty things to say to Charlotte.

I hadn't! Charlotte makes me sick. She's one of Madame Trikilnova's little pets. I decided to help Nikki out.

"Short hair is hot this year," I told Charlotte. "Of course, you wouldn't know. You have no style. They'd laugh you off the street in New York."

Charlotte's mouth dropped open.

So did Nikki's.

I smiled. I had given Charlotte just what she deserved.

"Let me have your attention," Pat called out. "Today is the day of the pointe demonstration I promised you. I want everyone to sit in a circle on the floor."

We all sat down.

I glanced around the circle.

Becky and Charlotte and Megan looked very excited.

Dean looked bummed out. I guess that was normal. Dean was probably disappointed we were taking time away from class to discuss pointe. (It's not exactly a boy thing.)

Philip looked happy to be getting out of dancing.

"I brought in several pairs of toe shoes," Pat announced. "You can pass these around."

When it was my turn to examine the shoes, I noticed the toes of some were harder than others. I wondered why, but I couldn't ask Pat. After all, I was supposed to know about this stuff. I was happy when Lynn raised her hand and asked the same question.

"The harder ones are for performing dances with more *pirouettes* in them," Pat explained.

"Cool," Becky said.

I thought so, too. But I just nodded as if it were old news to me.

"Does anyone know the name of the ballerina

who first danced on pointe?" Pat asked.

I shook my head. So did all the other kids.

"It was Marie Taglioni," Pat told us. "She was dancing the part of a fairy in a ballet called *La Sylphide*. She used toe shoes to create the illusion that she was flying. Does anyone know how long ago that was?"

"In the 1950s?" Risa suggested.

"No way!" Katie called out. "Dancing on pointe has been around longer than that. I bet it was three hundred years ago."

Pat laughed. "Not quite, Katie. Marie Taglioni first danced on pointe in 1832. That was about a hundred sixty years ago."

Risa stuck her tongue out at Katie.

Katie made a face at Risa.

"Do male dancers ever dance on pointe?" Pat asked us.

"No!" most of the class yelled out.

But John Stein waved his hand in the air.

"What do you think?" Pat asked John.

"Some boys dance on pointe in class," John said. "Once in a while my dad has his male students do exercises on pointe." John's father is a ballet instructor at our school.

Pat nodded. "Do you know why he does that?"

"It helps them strengthen their ankles," John said.

"That's right," Pat agreed.

"But only girls perform on pointe," John added.

"I can think of a ballet where a male dancer performs on pointe," Pat told him. "It's a modern ballet called *The Dream*. In it the character Bottom is magically turned into a donkey. The dancer who plays this part dances on pointe to create the impression of having animal's hooves."

"Are you going to dance on pointe for us?" Kim asked Pat.

"No," Pat said. "It takes years of preparation for a dancer to strengthen his or her ankles and legs enough to dance on pointe. After you begin, you have to practice regularly to keep your muscles strong. I haven't been dancing much since I broke my ankle, so my muscles are weak."

"Great demonstration," Becky mumbled, looking disappointed.

Pat smiled. "Not so fast," she told Becky. "I've invited a guest to class to demonstrate for you."

Just then we all heard the studio door open. We turned around to see who had come in. It was Heather McCabe, the best dancer from the advanced class. She looked nervous.

"Hi," Pat said, walking over to Heather and putting an arm around her. "We're all looking forward to seeing you dance."

"What do you want me to do?" Heather asked Pat.

"Do you know any dances?" Pat asked.

Heather nodded. "I know the Sugarplum Fairy's solo from *The Nutcracker*."

"Perfect," Pat said.

Heather did a few quick stretches. "I did barre exercises with my class, so I'm already warmed up," Heather told Pat. "I'm ready whenever."

Pat nodded to Al.

Megan smiled when the music started. "I love the music from *The Nutcracker*," she whispered to me.

Heather's nervousness disappeared when she started to dance. She did a beautiful *arabesque*. Her right foot was flat on the ground. Her left foot was raised up behind her. Holding the pose, Heather did a *relevé* onto pointe with her right foot. Then she lowered her foot so that it was flat on the ground again. She repeated the movement many times. It looked as if she was gliding across the studio.

"Wow," Becky breathed.

Heather did a series of rapid turns that took her from one side of the studio to the other. I was amazed. I was worried about doing a simple *pir-*

ouette, and Heather had just done at least fifteen difficult turns.

"She's incredible," Megan whispered to me.

I just nodded. I was watching Heather do a *pas de chat.* That's a kind of jump. We had already learned it in Pat's class. But Heather did the jump much better than any of us could. She really got off the ground.

When the music stopped, Heather took a tiny step back and smiled shyly.

Becky started applauding. We all joined in, even Pat. Even Al! I was impressed. Heather was a talented dancer.

"That was beautiful," Pat said. "Does anyone have any questions for Heather?"

"What's your favorite part of dancing on pointe?" Becky asked.

"It makes me feel like part of the music," Heather said.

Becky grinned. She looked starstruck.

"Do you get a lot of blisters?" Kim asked.

Heather laughed. "Tons!"

"Have you ever performed on pointe?" Lynn asked.

"Not yet," Heather said. "But at the recital this year, I'm going to dance with a boy in my class, Chris Adabo."

Megan and Nikki exchanged looks. They both think Chris Adabo is cute.

"Do you ever fall?" I asked.

"I try not to," Heather replied, looking serious. "A lot of dancers hurt themselves falling. When you're on toe, you have to be careful not to mess up your ankles."

Pat nodded solemnly. Then she said, "May I ask a question?"

"Sure," Heather said.

"Where did you learn the Sugarplum Fairy's dance?" Pat asked.

"I taught it to myself," Heather said. "See, I was Clara in *The Nutcracker* for two years. I saw the dance so many times in rehearsals and performances that I learned all the steps."

Pat winked at us. "Maybe one of you girls will be Clara in *The Nutcracker* this winter," she said.

All the girls in the class exchanged excited looks.

"I have to go," Heather told Pat. "Madame Trikilnova doesn't want me to miss too much of my class."

"Okay," Pat said. "Thanks for coming."

Heather gave us a little wave and ran out.

"She's really good," Lynn told Pat.

"I can't wait until I can dance that solo," Charlotte added.

"Well, please remember that all of you are several years away from starting pointe work," Pat said. "You're going to have to wait until you're at least eleven, probably twelve."

Why did Pat have to say that? She had just told everyone that I lied! I tried to look calm. But my stomach was tying itself in knots. I kept my head down so that none of the other girls could see my face.

"Some of the exercises we do in class, like *relevés*, will help you strengthen the muscles you will need later," Pat added. "Okay, let's do some dancing."

"Pat, wait," Katie called out. "I want to ask a question."

"Go ahead," Pat said.

Katie glanced at me. "Do any schools start girls on pointe when they're our age?" she asked.

"Some probably do," Pat said. "But a good school never rushes its students. Even though you guys are impatient, it really is better for you to wait."

Katie shot me an evil look.

I did my best to ignore her.

"Okay," Pat said. "We don't have much time

left. Let's try to get through the barre before class is over. Places!"

Everyone ran for the barre.

I didn't even try to concentrate on my *pliés* and *relevés*. I was too worried about what would happen when class ended. I was sure the other girls knew I was lying. I didn't think I could talk my way out of this.

"That's it for today," Pat announced way too soon.

Nikki walked up to Pat while we were still applauding. "Jillian studied pointe in New York," she said. "She even knows how to do a *pirouette*."

"Really?" Pat said, giving me a funny look. "That must have been exciting for you."

"It was," I said. "Well, I've got to get home. See you guys."

My heart was beating fast. I couldn't believe Pat hadn't given me away. But I wasn't safe yet. I hurried into the dressing room. Nikki, Katie, Risa, Becky, and Megan were right behind me.

I took a deep breath. If I wasn't going to blow this, I had to be calm.

Fourteen

Showdown

"Why don't you admit it?" Katie asked me. "We know you lied."

Katie, Nikki, Risa, Megan, and Becky had followed me to my locker. They all looked angry.

"I didn't lie," I insisted. "Pat said some schools start girls on pointe at our age. That's what happened to me."

"Pat also said a good school wouldn't start pointe so early," Risa pointed out. "And you're always telling us how great the School of American Ballet is."

"It's the best," I said. "And I studied pointe there."

"Pat seemed surprised when I told her that," Nikki reminded me.

I shrugged. "I guess Pat doesn't know everything."

"Prove it," Katie said.

"I will," I said. "I'll bring my toe shoes in and dance for you."

"You keep saying that," Risa told me. "But you never do it."

"I'll bring them on Thursday," I promised.

"And you're going to do a *pirouette*, right?" Katie asked.

"No problem," I said.

"I bet," Katie said.

"*I* bet you're going to owe me an apology," I said. "It's not nice to go around calling people liars."

"Unless it's true," Katie said.

"Don't fight!" Megan exclaimed. "We'll find out who's right on Thursday."

"Fine," Katie said. "Come on, you guys."

Katie and Risa headed for the door.

"Wait for me," Nikki said, hurrying after them.

Becky and Megan hung around a while longer. They seemed to be searching for something to say to me.

"Listen," Megan said at last. "I'm sorry about Risa and Katie and Nikki. They were acting like you were on trial or something."

I shrugged. "They weren't very nice."

"Well, you have been promising to bring the

shoes in for a long time," Becky pointed out. "I don't blame them for wondering what's taking so long."

"What *is* taking so long?" Megan asked.

I forced myself to smile. I had only been able to practice dancing on pointe that one time. But I was still pretty sure I would be able to dance well enough to fool the others. I was a little worried about the *pirouette,* but I told myself not to be.

"Just get here early on Thursday," I said to Becky and Megan. "You'll see for yourselves that I'm not lying."

Fifteen

Caught

"Jillian, may I speak to you for a moment?" Pat asked. She had poked her head out of Madame Trikilnova's office as I was leaving the ballet school.

"Sure," I said.

"Come in," Pat said.

I walked into the office. Pat pushed the door closed until it was open only a crack. She looked worried.

"Is everything okay with you and the other girls?" Pat asked.

My throat tightened up. I felt as if I was about to start crying. I shook my head.

Pat put an arm around my shoulder. "Don't worry," she told me. "It's going to be okay. Just tell me what happened."

I knew Pat wanted to help. But I couldn't get any words out.

"Did you tell the other girls you could dance on pointe?" Pat guessed.

I nodded.

Just then Pat looked up. She seemed startled.

I spun around. It was Madame Trikilnova! She had come into the office. I could tell she had heard Pat's question and seen me nod. Madame Trikilnova had a big ugly frown on her face.

"I'm sorry, Madame," Pat said. "I was just borrowing your office for a minute. I'll get out of your way now."

"It's too late for that, Miss Kelly," Madame Trikilnova said. "I already heard too much."

I started to cry. I could tell something awful was about to happen.

"Stop crying," Madame Trikilnova ordered me. "It doesn't help."

I sniffled. I tried to stop, but I couldn't. Once I start crying, I keep crying until I'm cried out.

Madame Trikilnova looked disgusted. "Lying is a bad habit," she told me. "I do not approve of it. I want you to tell the other girls the truth. And do not touch a pair of toe shoes until a teacher tells you that you're ready to do so."

While Madame Trikilnova made this speech, Pat kept opening her mouth and closing it without saying anything. She looked mad. But she must have thought it was smarter not to interrupt.

I was mad, too. And I was not afraid to speak up.

"You can't tell me what to do," I shouted at Madame Trikilnova.

"I most certainly can," Madame Trikilnova shot back. "This is my school. Do as I say. If you don't, you will not be welcome here any longer."

"Fine!" I yelled, storming out of the office.

I rushed down the stairs and threw open the front door. Before the door slammed behind me, I heard Madame Trikilnova and Pat start to argue.

Sixteen

A Dangerous Performance

"I want to thank you all for a great school year," Mr. Cosgrove said during our end-of-the-school-year party on Thursday. "You guys have taught me a lot. I hope you learned as much as I did. Have a terrific summer!"

Everyone in my class cheered.

Megan stood up. "We have something to give you," she told Mr. Cosgrove.

Dean pulled a box out of his desk. He and Megan carried it up to the front of the room together.

The other kids crowded forward as Mr. Cosgrove started to unwrap the present.

I hung back. I didn't feel like part of the celebration. I was much too nervous. Besides, Megan had told me what was in the box at the same time she had told me how much fun Becky's barbecue had been. It was a mug that said, WORLD'S BEST TEACHER.

I glanced at the clock. School would be over in a few minutes. Half of me wanted the day never to end. The other half wished it were already over. All I could think about was whether I would be able to fool Becky, Megan, Katie, Risa, and Nikki.

I sat down at my desk. I played with the cupcake sitting in front of me. I couldn't wait for this mess to be over.

"Do you think he liked it?"

I looked up. Megan and Becky were standing in front of my desk, smiling at me.

"Who?" I asked.

"Mr. Cosgrove," Becky said. "Do you think he liked his present?"

"Yes," I said.

Dean came up behind Megan. He pointed at my cupcake. "Aren't you going to eat that?" he asked.

"No," I said, handing it to him. I was too nervous to eat.

"I can't believe the school year is over," Megan said.

Becky spun around in a circle. "A whole summer of freedom," she said. "Yippee!"

"Not completely free," Megan said. "I'm going to take ballet this summer. Are you guys?"

"Yes," Becky said.

"If my parents let me," Dean said with his mouth full.

I nodded. Just then the final bell rang. Kids all over the school started screaming.

I stood up. "I'll see you at the ballet school," I told Megan and Becky. "Meet me in the dressing room."

"Where are you going?" Megan asked.

"Home to get my toe shoes," I explained.

"Hurry," Megan said.

"I will," I said. I took off at a run.

That morning I had decided not to bring the toe shoes to school for two reasons:

1. I didn't want my mother to discover they were gone. (She usually comes home for lunch.)

2. I didn't want people at school asking me questions about them all day.

The hallway at school was packed with kids who were hugging their friends and throwing papers up in the air. I pushed through the crowd as quickly as I could.

I ran all the way to my grandparents' house and sneaked inside. Everything was quiet. I went to Mom's room and took out the shoe box. The toe shoes were inside, just where I had left them. I stuffed them into my bag.

I was gone before Grandma realized I was

there. Darrow gave me a puzzled look as I let my-self out the front door.

I ran all the way to the ballet school. I knew that if I was late, if I made *any* excuse for not dancing on pointe that afternoon, the other girls would know I had been lying.

I got to the ballet school in about four minutes flat. Megan, Nikki, Becky, Risa, and Katie were waiting for me in the dressing room. Class wouldn't begin for almost thirty minutes.

"Did you bring them?" Katie demanded.

"Yes," I said, catching my breath.

The girls gathered around as I pulled the toe shoes out.

"They look brand-new," Risa commented.

"I got a new pair just before I left New York," I said.

"How come the ribbons don't match?" Katie asked.

"Uh—" I said. "Everyone wears them this way in New York. It's the latest style."

"The studio is open," Becky said. "I already checked. Come on. I want to see you dance before Lynn and Charlotte get here."

I thought that was a good idea. I didn't need a bigger audience than I already had. I wondered where Madame Trikilnova was. She could have been in her office or teaching the advanced class. I really didn't care where she was as long as she didn't come anywhere near Studio C.

The other girls had already changed. I put on my tights and leotard as quickly as possible. Then we all hurried up to the studio together.

I felt very nervous as I tied the toe shoes on and stood up in them. I held on to the barre and willed my legs to stop shaking. The other girls were watching every move I made.

I started to stretch out. I did a few *demi-pliés*.

"Hurry up," Risa told me. "Everyone will be coming soon."

"Okay," I said. "I guess I'm ready."

"Do a *relevé* first," Becky suggested.

As I did the *relevé*, I watched myself in the mirror. My legs looked great, but my face looked terrible. If I wasn't careful, everyone would know I was scared to death. I forced myself to smile.

I could see the other girls in the mirror, too. Becky and Megan were grinning at me. But the other girls' faces sent a shiver up my spine. They did not look friendly.

"What next?" I asked, trying to sound casual.

"*Bourrées*," Katie said.

I turned to face the barre. I held on to it with both hands and put my feet in fifth position. I did a *demi-plié* and then rose up onto pointe. I took a tiny step with my left foot and then my right foot. I did that over and over again. I moved slowly down the barre to the right. After I had gone about three feet, my toes were screaming out for relief. I came down.

The other girls did not look convinced.

"Do an *arabesque*," Risa suggested.

Great! I thought. I was happy to do anything that was not a *pirouette*.

I held on to the barre with my left hand. With my feet in fifth position I rose up on pointe. I did a *développé* to the back. At the same time, I lifted my right arm up in front. I balanced for as long as I could with just my left toes touching the floor.

"That was a nice *arabesque*," Megan said after I came down. She was grinning. "I knew you weren't lying."

"Well, I'm not so sure," Nikki said. "She hasn't done much."

"I'm just a beginner," I burst out. "What do you expect?"

"You said you could do a *pirouette*," Katie reminded me.

"Yeah," Becky said. "I want to see a *pirouette*."

My legs were starting to feel tired. The big toe on my left foot hurt. "I'm not sure I can do that," I admitted. "I haven't done one in a while."

Katie and Risa exchanged triumphant glances.

"They didn't teach you much at that fancy school," Risa said. "*Relevés*—big deal."

"Come on, Jillian," Megan said. "If you studied pointe, I'm sure you can do a *pirouette*. Do just one."

For half a second I considered confessing. But I decided it was too late for that.

My legs were beginning to shake. I took a bunch of deep breaths. I told myself that if I could do a *pirouette*—just one—the others would believe me.

Carefully I let go of the barre. I went into fourth position with my right foot back. Then I used my arms to give me the power to push up and turn onto my left leg.

As soon as my right foot left the ground, I knew something was wrong. I got up on pointe, but I was totally off balance. My left ankle wobbled. Then it gave out from under me. I felt a sharp pain. I screamed as I crashed to the floor.

Seventeen

Ouch!

"Are you okay?" Megan asked, rushing to my side.

Becky was right behind her.

"I'm fine," I said, getting up. But when I put weight on my left foot, a pain shot through my entire leg. I sat back down in a hurry.

"What's wrong?" Becky asked.

"My ankle hurts," I said.

Megan looked at my foot. "Wow," she said. "It's already swelling up."

"I'll get help," Katie said, darting toward the door.

Katie came back a few seconds later with Madame Trikilnova. I didn't think to take off my toe shoes before she came into the studio. She looked furious when she saw them on my feet.

"What happened here?" Madame Trikilnova asked.

"Jillian was dancing for us," Risa explained.

"She fell," Megan added. "I think she broke her ankle."

Without a word Madame Trikilnova bent down next to me. She gently pressed her fingers to my ankle. When she had finished her examination, she sat back and glared at me.

"You were dancing on pointe, no?" Madame Trikilnova asked me coldly.

I couldn't exactly lie. The evidence was on my feet. Besides, I was sick of lying.

"Yes," I whispered.

"You fool," Madame Trikilnova said fiercely. "You have no training on pointe and yet you insist on dancing! Why do you think I forbade you to do so?"

I stared back at her without answering. I could feel the tears starting to drip off of my chin.

"It is not simply because I am a nasty old woman," Madame Trikilnova threw out. "It is because I knew this would happen. I knew it. I should never have trusted you. Liars are not to be trusted."

Becky stared at Madame Trikilnova. She seemed stunned by the way Madame Trikilnova was yelling at me.

"You are such a faker," Nikki told me.

"Nikki," Megan said. "How can you say that now? Jillian is hurt!"

"She got what she deserved," Nikki said.

"Enough!" Madame Trikilnova said as she stood up. She seemed calmer now. "Jillian, take those shoes off your feet. I'm going to call your mother."

Madame Trikilnova left.

I tried to untie the ribbons on my toe shoes. But I was crying too hard. I couldn't see what I was doing. Katie came over to help me.

By the time Katie got the toe shoes off, Madame Trikilnova was back. "Your mother is meeting with a client in Seattle," she told me. "Your grandfather beeped her. She will meet us at the hospital."

"We'll help Jillian out to your car," Becky told Madame Trikilnova.

"Good," Madame Trikilnova said. "Get all of her belongings out of the dressing room, too."

Katie ran down to the dressing room. When she came back with my stuff, Becky helped me put a tennis shoe on my good foot. Megan let me lean on her as I hopped out to Madame Trikilnova's car.

It was almost time for class to start.

Pat arrived just as I was getting into the car. Megan told her what had happened.

"Are you okay, honey?" Pat asked me through the car window.

I nodded.

Pat and Al and most of the Pinks watched as

Madame Trikilnova and I drove off. Pat seemed worried. So did Al, Kim, Lynn, and all the boys. But Nikki looked furious. I couldn't guess what Megan, Becky, Risa, and Katie were thinking.

The closest hospital to Glory is halfway down the road toward Seattle. It's about a fifteen-minute drive. That afternoon it felt more like an hour.

I couldn't stop sobbing. My ankle hurt like crazy. But that wasn't what was upsetting me the most. Madame Trikilnova wouldn't say one word to me. I was desperate to make her understand my side of the story. I couldn't stand her disapproval any longer.

"Madame Trikilnova," I choked out. "I'm—I'm sorry."

"It's too late to apologize," she told me.

"But you don't understand—" I started.

"I'm not interested in your explanations," Madame Trikilnova said.

I stared out the car window. My tears made the trees and phone poles that were whizzing by blur. *You are such a faker*. That's what Nikki had said. She was right.

I could imagine what the other girls were saying about me now. I was sure I would never make friends in Glory.

Madame Trikilnova finally pulled up at the hospital.

"Stay here," she ordered me. "I'll be right back."

Madame Trikilnova got out of the car and walked quickly toward the building. She disappeared inside. I felt abandoned. But a few seconds later an attendant came out with a wheelchair. My mother appeared right behind him.

Mom rushed up to the car. "Are you okay?" she asked me.

"I think so," I said.

The attendant helped me into the wheelchair. Then he started to push me inside.

Mom took my hand as I rolled along. "Don't be afraid," she said. "I'm going to stay with you."

I gave Mom's hand a squeeze.

Hospitals are big places. This one was also very crowded. Mom and I had to wait to get my foot X-rayed. Then we had to wait for the X ray to be developed. Then we had to wait for a doctor to tell us what the X ray showed.

I had plenty of time to tell Mom the whole story about the toe shoes. I expected her to yell at me. But she didn't even get angry. She seemed sad and thoughtful. In a way, that was even worse. I knew I had disappointed her. And disappointment is much worse than anger.

Eighteen

Kicked Out

"It's just a bad sprain," the doctor told me and Mom as he studied the X rays. "All Jillian needs is a bandage and some aspirin."

"That's great news," Mom said.

"Will I be able to dance again?" I asked.

The doctor glanced at my tights and leotard. "Sure you will," he said, giving me a wink. "But not for the next two weeks."

"What a drag," I mumbled.

"You need to give your ankle time to heal," the doctor said firmly. "And that means no dancing for the next two weeks. Promise?"

"Promise," I told him.

Mom took one look at my downcast face and started to laugh. "It could have been much worse," she told me.

"I know," I said.

After we were finished with the doctor, Mom gathered up my stuff. The doctor had given me a cane. I practiced using it as we headed toward the exit.

When we got back to the waiting room, we discovered that Madame Trikilnova was still there.

Mom rushed over to her. I stayed as far away as possible.

"You didn't have to wait!" Mom told Madame Trikilnova. "But I'm glad you did. Now I have an opportunity to thank you for driving Jillian over."

Mom motioned for me to join them. I went to stand next to her. She put her arm around my shoulders.

"Jillian is going to be fine," Mom told Madame Trikilnova. "She'll be back in class before you know it."

"That's what I want to talk to you about," Madame Trikilnova said. "I've been waiting for you so that I could let you know."

Mom raised her eyebrows. "Let me know what?" she asked.

"There is one week left in the spring session," Madame Trikilnova said. "I would prefer it if Jillian did not register for any more classes after that."

"What are you saying?" Mom asked.

"Jillian is no longer welcome at my school," Madame Trikilnova said.

Madame Trikilnova can't kick me out, I told myself. *It isn't fair!* I had to bite my tongue to stop myself from saying it out loud. (Sometimes it's better to let grown-ups argue things out themselves.)

"May I ask why?" Mom said in her lawyer voice.

Madame Trikilnova made a prune face. "Because she's vain, irresponsible, and a bad influence on the other girls," she said.

A woman sitting nearby peeked at us over her magazine. We were creating a scene. But I was too upset to worry about that. Tears were welling up in my eyes.

"Madame Trikilnova," my mother protested. "I don't see—"

"You have heard my decision," Madame Trikilnova interrupted. "It's final." She turned to leave.

"Do something," I whispered to Mom.

Mom looked down and studied my face for a moment. "Hold on a second!" she called after Madame Trikilnova.

Madame Trikilnova stopped walking. She turned around and faced my mother.

"I admit that what Jillian did was wrong," Mom said. "She's not perfect."

Madame Trikilnova was listening. She was even nodding! She probably liked hearing my mother say how rotten I was. *I* didn't like it much.

"However, I cannot agree with your decision to kick Jillian out of your school," Mom went on. "I

think she deserves a second chance."

"I'm not so sure," Madame Trikilnova said.

"*Everyone* deserves a second chance," Mom insisted. She took a deep breath. "If you won't give one to Jillian, give one to me."

"To you?" Madame Trikilnova asked.

My mother nodded. "You see, I think Jillian's behavior is partly my fault," she said. "My husband and I recently divorced. Then I dragged Jillian all the way across the country. She's been through a lot."

Madame Trikilnova didn't say anything.

"Oh, have a heart," Mom said. "She's just a kid!"

"Madame Trikilnova," I said carefully. "Please don't throw me out. I promise I won't ever disobey you again."

Madame Trikilnova sighed. "Oh, all right," she said. "I will give you another chance. But I'm warning you, I am going to be watching you."

"Okay," I said. "That's fine! Thanks."

As soon as Madame Trikilnova was gone, I threw my arms around my mother's neck. "You were great!" I said.

Mom and I went outside. She pulled the car around and helped me get in.

I studied my mother's face as she started to drive. She looked tired and sad. I knew that was partly my fault. It did not make me feel good.

"I'm sorry I said that I hated you," I told Mom quietly. "I don't."

Mom smiled. "I know the last few months have been hard for you, Jill," she said.

"Don't call me—" I started. But then I bit my tongue. I didn't want to start a fight.

"Oops," Mom said, glancing at me. "I slipped again. Sorry, *Jillian*."

"It's not a big deal," I said.

"Maybe not," Mom said. "But I still want to get it right."

"Thanks," I whispered. I'm not sure why, but I was starting to cry again. Maybe it was because Mom was being so nice.

Mom sneaked a look at me. "Do you hate it here?" she asked, turning her eyes back to the road.

"Nooo," I said slowly. I didn't sound very convincing—not even to myself. I only said no because I didn't want to hurt Mom's feelings. I think she knew that.

"Is there anything I can do to make life here easier for you?" Mom asked.

"The mailbox," I said without thinking.

"What?" Mom asked.

I could feel my face grow hot. "The mailbox," I repeated. "I'd like you to put my name on the mailbox."

"I think that could be arranged," Mom said. But she sounded puzzled.

I tried to explain. "It would make me feel like I belong here. Right now I feel like a Kormach just visiting a house full of Bells."

"I see," Mom said. "Well, we can't have that. We'll have to repaint the mailbox right away."

"Great," I said. *That* had been easy. I wiped the tears off my face. "I might think of more things later."

Mom laughed. "Okay. Let me know."

"Don't worry," I said. "I will!"

"I'm happy you want to go back to the ballet school," Mom told me. "But I'm a little surprised you feel that way. Facing the other girls is going to be hard."

"I know," I said. "But staying away would have been harder. I would miss dancing *so* much."

I sat without speaking for a few minutes. I was starting to feel sorry for myself.

"Things at the ballet school won't change that much," I added at last. "Nobody there ever liked me anyway."

"Don't worry," Mom said. "You'll make friends soon."

I nodded and tried to smile. But people had been telling me that ever since Mom and I moved to Glory. I just didn't believe it anymore.

Nineteen

A First Step

Ruff! Rrr-ruff!

Whenever our doorbell rings, Darrow and Marshall go crazy. They bark and jump up against the door.

The doorbell rang that evening after dinner. We had finished eating, but we were still sitting around the table.

"I wonder who that could be," Grandma said.

"I'll find out," I said. I limped into the front hall as fast as I could. (Which was not very fast.) I pulled the dogs back and opened the door.

Pat was standing on the front porch.

"Hi," I said, surprised. "What are you doing here?"

"I came to check on your ankle," Pat said. She held out a gallon of ice cream. "I also brought you this."

120

I took the ice cream and opened the door wider. "Come in."

"Thanks," Pat said. "How's your ankle?"

"It's just sprained," I told her.

"Who is it, Jillian?" Mom asked, coming into the hallway.

"My ballet teacher," I answered.

A shadow passed over my mother's face. I almost giggled. I had a feeling Mom expected Pat to be as difficult as Madame Trikilnova.

"This is my mother," I told Pat. "Mom, this is Pat."

Pat extended a hand. "Hello, Mrs. Kormach," she said. "I want you to know what a pleasure it has been for me to have Jillian in my class. She always works very hard."

Mom broke into a grin. She came forward to shake Pat's hand. "My name isn't Mrs. Kormach," she said. "It's Ms. Bell. But why don't you call me Ann?"

"Okay," Pat agreed.

I held out the ice cream. "Pat brought this," I told Mom.

"Mmm, Butter Pecan is one of my favorites," Mom said, taking the container. "Why don't you come in and have a bowl with us?"

"I'd love to," Pat agreed.

Mom showed Pat into the living room.

121

Grandma and Grandpa came out to meet her.

I helped Mom dish up the ice cream. Then we all sat down together.

Pat asked a hundred questions about my ankle. "I'm glad it's only a sprain," she told us when she had heard the whole story. "I was worried it might have been broken."

"Pat broke her ankle last year," I explained to Mom and my grandparents.

"That's too bad," Mom said.

Pat nodded. "Some good has come of it. I learned that I love to teach." Pat turned to me. "I want to tell you a secret. I was doing something I shouldn't have been doing when I broke my ankle."

"You were?" I asked.

Pat nodded. "I was getting ready to perform an important *pas de deux* and—"

"An important *what*?" Grandpa interrupted.

"Grand-*pa*," I said. "A *pas de deux* is a dance for two people—usually a man and a woman."

"Is that right?" Grandpa asked Pat.

"That's right," she said with a grin.

"Go on, dear," Grandma told Pat.

"My partner was recovering from the flu," Pat continued. "He was going to be fine for the performance, but I didn't think we had rehearsed enough. I talked him into practicing one evening when we both knew he was too weak. It was stupid."

"What happened?" Grandpa asked.

"He dropped me," Pat said. "I paid a big price for being so impatient."

I smiled at Pat. "Well, I don't mind waiting a little longer to start pointe."

Pat winked at me. "Smart girl," she said.

I was starting to feel happier. Maybe going back to class wouldn't be so bad. Pat would never let the other girls be mean to me.

A few minutes after Pat left, the doorbell rang again. My ankle was starting to hurt, so I let Grandpa get it.

I was surprised when Megan came into the living room. I wondered if she had come to yell at me for lying to her.

When my family saw Megan, they hurried into the kitchen. They were trying to give us some privacy. I wasn't sure I wanted it.

"Hi, Megan," I said, feeling embarrassed.

"Hi," Megan answered. She looked uncomfortable. There was a long silence.

"I'm sorry I acted like such a jerk," I said at last.

"You weren't a jerk," Megan said. "Besides, it was my fault, too."

"Your fault?" I repeated. "Why would you think that?"

"It was my idea for you to bring the toe shoes to class," Megan said.

"I had already lied to you and Becky by then," I reminded Megan.

"That's the part I don't understand," Megan said. "Why did you tell me and Becky that you could dance on pointe?"

"I wanted to get your attention," I said. "I haven't made any friends since I moved to Glory. Nobody here likes me."

"That's not true," Megan told me.

"It is so," I said.

"Well . . . a lot of people think you're a snob," Megan said.

"I'm not a snob!" I yelled.

"*I* don't think you are," Megan told me. "But some kids don't like the way you brag about New York all the time."

I groaned. "I thought being from New York would make people like me," I said. "Sometimes I'm so stupid."

"Listen," Megan said. "Do you want to come to a slumber party at my house? It's on Saturday."

My jaw dropped. "Are you sure you want to invite me?" I asked. "Your friends might not want me there. Especially Nikki. She was really mad at me this afternoon."

"I'm sure," Megan insisted.

"Okay," I agreed. "I'll come."

After Megan had gone home, I promised myself I wouldn't do anything at the party to make the other girls hate me. I wouldn't lie. And I wouldn't talk about New York.

I was nervous. What if I got to the party, and everyone was mean to me? I knew I had to go anyway. It was one last chance for me to make friends in Glory.

Twenty

Clean Start

"How does that look?" Mom asked me.

I grinned. "Much better!"

Mom and I were standing in front of my grand-parents'—oops, I mean, *my* house. We were admiring the mailbox. Mom had a blotch of yellow paint on her nose and a big smile on her face.

We had been painting for more than an hour. First Mom had carefully lettered my name onto the box. Then she had suggested that I paint a few flowers. When I finished, Mom decided *she* wanted to add a few more. After that, things kind of got out of hand. I painted the New York City skyline. (At least, I *tried*.) Mom added birds and trees and mountains.

"You can hardly recognize the old box," Mom said.

"The letter carrier is going to freak out," I said.

Mom glanced at her watch. "Hey, it's getting late," she told me. "You had better get ready for your party. I'll clean up here."

"Thanks, Mom," I said. "Not just for cleaning up—I mean, thanks for painting the mailbox. Thanks for everything."

Mom smoothed back my hair and gave me a kiss on the forehead. "You're welcome, Jillian."

Twenty minutes later I knocked on Megan's door. I had no idea how the other girls were going to treat me. I hadn't seen any of them—except for Megan—since the day I fell.

"Hi, Jillian!" Megan said as she threw open the door.

"Hi," I said. "My grandmother made these brownies for us."

"Yummy," Megan said. "Come on in."

Megan led me down a hallway and into the den. Becky, Risa, and Katie were already there. They were playing a video game.

"Jillian's here," Megan announced. "She brought brownies."

"Great," Becky said.

Just then the doorbell rang.

"I'd better get that," Megan said, giving me an uncertain look. She headed back toward the front door.

I felt like running after Megan. I was more comfortable with her around. But I forced myself to stay where I was.

"Megan told us your ankle isn't broken," Becky said.

"No, it's just a sprain," I said.

"When will you be able to dance again?" Risa asked.

"In two or three weeks," I said.

There was a long silence. I imagined it lasting all night. I had to say something!

"I almost wasn't allowed to come back at all," I finally blurted out.

"Why not?" Risa asked.

"Madame Trikilnova wanted to kick me out of the ballet school," I said.

Risa and Becky looked surprised.

Katie rolled her eyes. "Madame Trikilnova is a big pain," she said.

"You're just mad because she yelled at you," Becky said. "I told you that you were going to get in trouble for being late to class all the time."

"It's not just that," Katie argued. "I never liked her."

"Well, I think she's great," Becky said.

Risa shook her head. "Katie and Becky are always fighting about Madame Trikilnova," she told me. "Why did she try to kick you out?"

"Yeah," Becky said. "What happened?"

I told them all about it. Megan came back with Nikki just as I was starting the story.

"Your mother must be super brave," Becky said when I finished. "My mom would never stand up to Madame Trikilnova. She's afraid of her."

"Mom is brave," I said.

"Jillian is brave, too," Nikki spoke up.

I stared at Nikki. She had said something nice about me! I was surprised.

"What are you talking about?" Katie asked Nikki.

"The other day in class, Charlotte was making fun of my hair," Nikki said. "Jillian totally put her in her place."

"I couldn't help it," I explained. "Charlotte makes me sick sometimes."

"Me too," Nikki told me. "Thanks for standing up for me."

I glanced around the circle of girls. Everyone looked more friendly now. I started to relax.

"Nikki!" I suddenly exclaimed. "What are you doing here? I thought you were grounded."

"Yeah," Katie said. "What's up?"

"You're not going to believe this," Nikki told us. "I had an appointment today with my modeling agency

129

in Seattle. My mom was freaking out all morning. She kept telling me the people at the agency were going to say I couldn't model until my hair grew back. But when we finally got to the agency, they loved my haircut! They kept telling my mother how fabulous I looked and what a genius she was. I threatened to tell them the truth unless she ungrounded me."

Everyone laughed.

I took a deep breath. "I'm sorry that I lied to all of you," I said.

The other girls looked surprised. I *had* changed the subject kind of quick. But I had to say it fast before I chickened out.

Katie recovered first. "Why did you do it?" she asked.

"I don't know," I told her. "I guess—I've been lonely since I moved to Glory. I was trying to make friends."

"I remember when I first moved to Glory," Risa said. "I was miserable for almost a year."

"It's hard to move," Nikki agreed. "Especially from someplace cool like New York City."

Becky turned to me. "Tell us more about New York," she said.

Uh-oh! I had promised myself I wasn't going to talk about that. "You don't want to hear about New York," I said.

"Yes, we do," Katie said.

The other girls nodded.

"Okay," I agreed. What else could I do? "What do you want to know?"

"Did you ever ride the subway?" Risa asked.

"Sure!" I said. "My baby-sitter used to take me to ballet class on the subway. It's really exciting. Millions of people ride it every day—" I stopped. I had suddenly realized I wasn't just talking, I was *bragging*.

"The subway isn't all great, though," I added quickly. "Especially in the summer. The stations get super hot."

"Have you been to the top of the World Trade Center?" Becky asked.

"My class used to go every year," I told her. "They have elevators that go so fast, it hurts your ears."

"Have you ever seen anyone famous?" Nikki asked.

"Dancers," I told her.

"Do you mean onstage?" Becky asked.

"Well, I have seen lots onstage," I said. "But I meant on the street or at my old ballet school."

"Who have you seen?" Becky asked.

"Baryshnikov," I said.

Becky's jaw dropped. "You're kidding me!" she yelled. "What did he look like?"

"Short," I said.

"That's it?" Becky demanded. "Short?"

I laughed. "He's handsome. He looks strong and smart."

"Wow," Becky breathed.

"Who else?" Nikki asked.

"Peter Martins used to come to my class," I said.

"He's the director of the New York City Ballet," Becky told the others.

"What was that like?" Katie asked.

"Scary," I said. "Just like when Madame Trikilnova comes to our class."

Everyone laughed.

"Have you ever seen Amanda McKerrow?" Megan asked.

It would have been easy for me to lie. But I was finished with that. "No, I haven't," I admitted.

Megan looked disappointed. But I was still glad I had told her the truth.

Katie jumped up. She pulled my toe shoes out of her overnight bag and handed them to me. "You left these at the ballet school," she explained. "I kept them for you."

"Thanks," I said, taking the shoes from her. "I forgot all about these. I guess I won't be needing them anymore."

"You should keep them," Becky said. "We'll be

starting pointe pretty soon. They might still fit you then."

"You think we'll be starting pointe soon?" Katie asked. "Since when is three years from now *soon*?"

"Three years will go by quickly," Megan said, defending Becky.

Katie shook her head. "You guys are crazy," she said.

"Well, one thing's for sure," Megan said. "It's going to be cool when we do start."

"Especially since we'll all be doing it together," I added.

Katie smiled. "What should we do now?" she asked.

"What do kids in New York do at slumber parties?" Megan asked me.

I didn't have to think about that for long. "We have dance contests," I said.

"That sounds like fun," Becky said.

"What do we do?" Megan asked.

"Well, first we have to pick partners," I said.

"I'll be your partner," Megan told me.

Becky said the same thing at the same time!

I started to laugh. I felt happier than I had in months. My long wait was over. I had made friends in Glory at last.

Pirouette

The Five Basic Positions

First position

Second position

Third position

Fourth position

Fifth position

WHAT THE BALLET WORDS MEAN

Arabesque (a-ra-BESK) A pose in which you balance on one leg, stretch the other out behind you, and hold your arms in a graceful position. There are many different kinds of *arabesques*.

Bourrées (boo-RAYS) A series of tiny steps that make a dancer look as if she is gliding across the floor.

Changement (shahnzh-MAHN) A move in which you jump up with one leg in front and land with the other leg in front.

Demi-plié (de-MEE plee-AY) A half knee-bend.

Demi-pointe (de-MEE pwahnt) Half-pointe. When a dancer is on *demi-pointe,* she is standing on the balls of her feet.

Développés (dayv-law-PAY) An exercise in which the dancer slowly stretches out her leg.

Pas de chat (pah duh shah) means "step of the cat" in French. It's a traveling step that looks a lot like a cat pouncing on a mouse.

Pas de deux (pah duh duh) Dance for two, usually a man and a woman.

Pas de bourrée (pah duh boo-RAY) A traveling step.

Pirouette (peer-oo-ET) is French for "whirl." It's a kind of turn in which the dancer spins around on one foot.

Plié (plee-AY) is a knee bend.

Pointe Dancing on pointe means dancing on your toes. Ballet dancers use special shoes to dance on pointe. Girls start dancing on their toes when they are about twelve. Before then, their bones are too soft.

Positions Almost every step in ballet begins and ends with the dancer's feet in one of five positions. The positions are called first, second, third, fourth, and fifth. The drawing on p. 135 shows how the positions look. Some ballet instructors use French words to describe the positions: *première, seconde, troisième, quatrième,* and *cinquième.*

Relevé (ruhluh-VAY) An exercise in which you rise up on the balls of your feet.

Tendus (tahn-DEW) An exercise in which you stretch one foot along the floor without bending your knees. Also called *battements tendus*.

Toe shoes Special shoes dancers wear to rise up on their toes. The toe area of the shoe is hard. Also called pointe shoes.

Tombé (tom-BAY) means "fall" in French. This is a movement in which the dancer falls onto one leg and bends her knee.

ABOUT THE AUTHOR

Emily Costello was born in Cincinnati, Ohio, and now lives in New York City. She likes to eat spaghetti, play tennis, and see movies. She has two left feet but enjoys watching ballet.